# Marooned

## WITH MY

# Celebrity

# Boss

# CONTENTS

# BLURB

*A thief on the run, and a celebrity actress looking for a fresh start.*

The name's Jasper Night, and I'm a thief—but not one of those criminals. I steal to survive, only taking stuff people don't want. Well...except for that one time I accidentally robbed a pirate.

A pirate who now wants to kill me.

So, I'm running.

Right into a cry-baby female who got in my way.

Okay, maybe I thought she was beautiful, but she was still in my way.

When I learned she owned a boat, she quickly became my plan to disappear. I convinced her to hire me as a ship captain. Now, she's my boss. It was all just too easy, until...we crashed into a deserted island.

*Marooned with My Celebrity Boss is a fake amnesia, soul mates, sweet romantic comedy with Aladdin vibes.*

To Bonnie R. I had asked in my reader group for a fun name for an island, and she delivered. I was going to use something easy like soulmate island, but she suggested Nuvola. It's Italian and means beyond the clouds, like somewhere over the rainbow. How could I not pick that? Thank you, Bonnie!

# One

## Evie



*Here we go. I pinch back a smile as it's the start of one of the happiest memories of my life.*

A tinted burst of light filtered through the stained-glass windows, casting colorful rainbow beams on the nearby wooden pews. Fresh blush rose petals lined the center aisle, decorating the path to the altar. As the organist struck her first chord, Elizabeth's three magenta-clad bridesmaids paired off with their groomsmen and strolled down the aisle, two by two.

I held back, waiting for my turn to walk, just before my sister. I couldn't stop smiling as I was so proud of my little baby sister. Just four years younger, she seemed to grow up right on my heels, following me around like a little pet. I'm not surprised she's the first to get married. She was a hopeless romantic, the opposite of me. She spent her days playing house, and pushing around little baby dolls, while I had spent my life—literally since I was four years old—working on television sets. I always knew she'd get her happy-ever-after relationship. I smiled wistfully at all the memories.

The last of the three bridesmaids made it down the aisle, and it was now my turn. Me, the maid of honor. I smoothed out the bustling hideous skirt that Elizabeth made me wear—fuchsia in color and with ruffles. I had begged her to let me wear something less colorful, but she insisted today had to be a "bright day" for us in all the ways. I tossed a look back at my sister, tucked between both of our parents as they waited for their turn down the aisle. She smiled warmly at me, her face radiating all the blessings she was gaining with her new life with Hank.

I raised my bouquet of magenta and blush roses, hooked my free arm with Hank's twin brother, Harold, and together we paced forward. Harold was shorter than me by a good three inches, and the very top of his head was bald, with glimmery sheen. I tried to fight it, but my eyes kept sliding over to study it. Not sure if that was due to a waxing situation or what, but I'd never seen such a shiny bald head before, and under the soft church lighting, it reflected sparkles. It was oddly beautiful.

*Eyes forward, Evie. It's rude to stare at his head.*

I pinned my gaze forward as Harold and I approached the altar, and then we parted to take our spots, waiting for Elizabeth. The music switched to the traditional wedding march, and the crowd rustled as everyone rose to their feet.

My heart thumped with happiness. Both my parents walked my sister down the aisle. Mom had big hair, reminiscent of 90s updo (even though we left the 90s thirty years ago), and she modeled a nice mother-of-the-bride, beige dress. Dad donned a formal tux, with magenta tie. I really do think Elizabeth took this magenta thing too far, but everyone willingly did it for her.

Elizabeth glided, her nine-foot, silk train—*that I paid for because they didn't have the money for their dream wedding, and I wanted the very best for her*—trailed behind her. Tears pricked the backs of my eyes as I couldn't take my eyes off her.

I was overflowing with pride.

Elizabeth hugged both my parents, and they took a seat in the front pew while Elizabeth joined Hank, whose eyes were glued to her. It was the sweetest thing to see my sister be so loved.

Father Jon made the sign of the cross and began to pray. Just as I bowed my head, a loud commotion came from the back of the church, and an imposing barrage of cameras rose in my peripheral vision, all aimed at *me*.

*My absolute worst nightmare.*

*Paparazzi.*

At least half a dozen seemed to pour out of the woodwork. I had no idea how they even got into this private ceremony. One started taking photos, and they all followed. The guests started to buzz, and a few people shouted at the party crashers to get out. My jaw dropped at the despicable behavior, and my joyful heart pitters shifted to a lower gear, thumping out anxiety.

Did they have no respect?

I didn't know how to stop it without shouting, and I certainly didn't want to make a scene. I cut a glance toward Elizabeth, her pleasant smile had fallen. Thankfully, the ushers made their way up front, but by now with so much stirring, the whole place was in an uproar. They pulled the photographers out by their forearms, but the wedding crashers laughed their way down the aisle. The arched wooden doors slammed behind them, echoing into the cathedral, and finally a heavy silence was restored in the church.

With a giant sigh of relief, I turned back to Elizabeth, ready to give her a weary smile, but her angry gaze was locked on me. Her dark golden brow lowered, and she planted her feet shoulder width apart. Her stance startled me so much, my head jolted back. I started to stutter out an apology, but she cut me off with a storm of words. "I hate you!" She screamed, planting a palm on her hip, sharply angling her elbow. "Just for once, can you let someone else have the spotlight! It's *my* wedding!"

Desperation filled my lungs, and before I could say anything, Harold had stepped out of line, hooked my arm again, and started to pull me back up the aisle.

"That's right," Elizabeth screamed after me. "Leave. You don't even deserve to be here. I never want to see you again. You just ruined the most important day of my life!"

"Let it go. It's not about you today," he whispered but it wasn't that whispery, and I'm sure everyone heard it.

*Not about me!*

*I never made it all about me. I was here to support her! It's not my fault the paparazzi had snuck in. They follow me everywhere. She can't blame me for this!*

My feet were unmoving bricks, and Harold used force to drag me away from my sister. It was probably for the best because if I had spoken, I would have told everyone how horrible this family really is.

How my parents had used me since I was a child, forcing me to go to every audition. For years, they stole my money to supplement their lifestyle, going on vacations without me, while I worked. My mom spent every penny she had. When there wasn't money left over for groceries, I'd bail her out with my money. A ten-year-old shouldn't have to put food on the table. I did it because inside I was suffering the loss of my childhood, and I wanted to ensure that at least one of us, Elizabeth, could have that perfect carefree innocence.

*I even paid for this whole wedding!*

I bit hard on my bottom lip, allowing Harold to pull me up the aisle. My eyes fixed on his gleaming bald spot like it was a flashing yellow caution light, guiding me to a safe exit.

Maybe it was time.

Nothing I could say would ever make my family see the sacrifices I'd made for them, and the lack of appreciation they'd given me. If they could honestly sit there and be silent when Elizabeth screamed her hatred at me, then I didn't need them.

It *was* finally time.

I'd dreamed of this moment for so many years. When I got to a point where I could walk away from all their drama and controlling ways to start my own life, free of them. This was the final straw. I jerked my arm back from Harold, dug my heels down to pick up my pace, speeding past him. "I can see myself out, thank you."

I didn't need to formulate a plan because I'd been fantasizing about my getaway for years. I was truly leaving my family, and this entire country behind. I'd go by sea; on the yacht I bought last year with my own hard-earned money. Once I get out to sea, nobody would be able to reach me. I would finally be freed of my mooching parents and ungrateful sister.

I picked up my pace, steadying myself on the slippery marble and raced out the front door.

*To the yacht, where my new life awaits!*

# Two

# Jasper

I was awakened by the sound of heavy military combat boots on the dock. It would only be a moment before the thugs would find me in my gondola. I'd been running for days, and even though I had found respite in a nap, they had caught up with me.

Again.

I shot to my feet as I was prepared, not scared—okay, maybe my heart felt as if it was going to beat right out of my chest, but anxiety is normal these days. I grabbed my tattered, leather satchel, where I stored all my earthly possessions, and tied it around my waist. Diving over the side, I made like a sea otter, swimming deep under water—all former signs of me dissipated.

It was just too easy.

You might be wondering why I was running from thugs. To best bring you up to speed, let's say I had an unconventional job. You remember Robin Hood, right? A nobleman who stole from the rich and gave to the poor. Well, it was something like that. I stole from the rich and gave to the poorest of the poor—*me*.

Before you wag your finger at me, I'm going to set something straight. I was one of those orphan kids who nobody loved, and then aged out of the system three years ago. With only myself to rely on, I couldn't afford fancy schooling, so I fixed up a busted gondola which had been discarded for trash. Now I spend my days carting around wealthy tourists. Those fancy Nancys don't always tip, so I filled in the gaps, flexing the petty thievery skills I had picked up in my youth. A day-old bagel here, a bottle of water there. Most people gladly looked the other way, and it meant I wouldn't starve to death. However, my story gets interesting after I picked the pocket of the wrong guy.

How was I to know he was a pirate? Or that he had a real treasure map stowed in his wallet. He did not have the proper peg leg, or hook hand to warn me. To me, he was another man lost in a sea of people. I got the find of a lifetime—an authentic treasure map— then made my escape.

Or so I thought.

Now his thugs were hot on my trail. Which is why I had a thoroughly thought out, and perfectly meticulously bulleted action plan—RUN!

Well, at the current moment, it was more of a swimming action, but it had the exact same thesis. I power stroked so hard ol' Henry Ford would have been proud, until I couldn't hold my breath for a microsecond longer. Gasping for air, I eased my head up, eyes peeled, and I found...nothing.

Sweet bliss.

I was on the south end of the docks where all the rich people berthed their huge boats. Perfect place for me to hide, because big boats cast big shadows. And, as any good thief would know, big boats also meant there'd likely be supplies I could use. Starting with a change of clothes. I slopped my feet up on the docks, and sloshed forward, feeling the squish of my clothes against my toned-body-builder physique—okay, maybe I had a few extra pounds, but they helped keep me warm on nights I had to sleep outside.

Casing the area with the stealth of a panther, I quickly realized the docks were quiet. Creepily, eerily, quiet, which wasn't exactly good, because it meant I had to be quieter as I sloshed since there was no crowd for me to blend into. The docks may have been empty due to the forecasted storm. High winds rolled through the alleys in between the boats, creating their own little wind tunnels. My teeth chattered so strongly, I felt the reverberations in my toes, but I kept moving because I'd be found if I didn't. My only goal now was to find the treasure before they found me. The unfortunate part was I needed to get to an island a short jaunt from here, and my gondola couldn't handle these seas. My eyes roved over the moored boats.

My lips curled into a devilish grin as I narrowed in on the boat I would steal. You might think I loved this boat because it was the biggest, or the most expensive. Touché. I stayed away from the biggest boats. They tended to have the best alarm systems. The yacht I had my eye on was the runt of this litter. I also loved it because it was on the far end of the dock where the light barely reached. There were plenty of shadows for me to hide in, and a window near the wheelhouse door that would give me access. Rubbing my hands together, my adrenaline building, I was about to make my move when a rustle from behind alerted me.

Ah, *shoot!*

I wasn't alone.

A woman was standing on the dock, crying.

Staying cool, I gave her my best Jack Sparrow gaze. Luckily for me, she looked away. I was safe—for now.

But not if she didn't shut up! She was crying louder than a hungry newborn, and I didn't need any noise rockets blasting out my whereabouts.

"Psst." I harshly blew in her direction. "Do you mind crying more quietly?"

Nothing but soap opera sobs.

"Hey, lady," I screeched, while tossing a security check over my shoulder. "You have got to be quiet."

She sniffed. "It's a free dock, and I can cry if I want." Her eyes narrowed after sizing me up and she continued to assert, "It's really none of your business if I can't stop crying. Besides I'm more mad crying than sad crying at his point. My whole family is ridiculous because they hate me for something I didn't even do."

"Er. It can't be that bad," I offered, not understanding why I was getting sucked into her personal problems. "I'm sure you didn't do anything on purpose." My eyes scanned the docks, which were thankfully still empty. I'd been on the run constantly for a week, and there was no way those thugs would stop now. I couldn't stop moving, but I also couldn't hijack a boat with this crybaby standing there. "Well, then maybe go home because a storm's coming."

"My sister told me to stay away from her forever. So, I'm going to. I was going to take my boat out, but my captain said it's too dangerous." Finally lifting her chin toward me, her eyes washed over me, her forehead dimpled. "Hey, why are you all wet?"

I started to stutter out an excuse, but I had a lightning bolt slam into my brain, flashing two words: GOLDEN TICKET! With a treasure map burning a hole in my satchel, and thugs on my tail, this was exactly the break I was waiting for. I leaned on the dock rail with swagger, hiked an Elvis brow, and gave her my best sell. "Why, I'm a ship captain and I was just diving to look underneath my boat to inspect the keel." Holding out my hand in a noble gesture, I flashed her my dashing lady-killer smile. "The name is Jasper. Nice to meet you."

She received my hand, letting her eyes meet mine, and I took in the sight of her. Oddly, she's not dressed for sailing. She is adorned in a ball gown fit for a princess, disheveled dark hair, and mascara tears trailing down her cheek, it was clear her night hadn't gone the way she had planned. She sniffed back another tear as her shoulders quivered. She pushed through it and managed to squeak out, "You can call me, Evie."

"Evie." I gently squeezed her hand, letting her name ring in my ear because something about her seemed familiar. Her skin was so fair, you'd think it had never been touched by the sun, and not a freckle or spot anywhere in sight. Her eyes were dark, and though swollen from crying, they looked pained, like she was in agony so deep, it made me want to whisper. I managed to ask in a normal voice, "Do I know you from somewhere?"

The smile she was beginning to form on her lips instantly faded. "You have probably seen me on TV. I'm sure I'm unrecognizable with my make-up all messed up, but my real name is Evelynn Darling, the actress."

Since I'd spent the entirety of my adult life homeless, I didn't know much about TV. Even when I was in the orphanage, we didn't have the freedom to watch whatever we wanted. I mused at the suggestion, reckoning it could have been possible I'd seen some show in passing with her in it. Shrugging, still unconvinced, but willing to move past the question at hand, I added, "I don't watch TV, but perhaps." A knot in my stomach wrenched, reminding me I was wasting precious time. I wanted to come off as professional, so I didn't rush my offer when I changed the subject back. "I ah, might be able to help you take your boat out."

"Really? You know how to pilot a yacht?" Her eyes brightened as they continued to hold mine. "There's a storm, but I looked at the radar. If we left now, we could sail around it and wait it out at sea."

Not wanting to seem too eager and make her suspicious, I started to coin a helpful-but-hesitant reply, but a flicker of light at the end of the dock stole my attention. Shadows were moving fast, and my senses told me the thugs were running this way. I couldn't take my chances standing here, playing a game. I pinned on a gracious smile. "Well, I can certainly try." I motioned to the row of boats. "Why don't we board your boat, so I can take a look?"

"First, I need to check your references." Her eyes glittered back at me now. Instead of walking forward, her feet cemented to the planks, making my heart rate ramp up because I could see the shadows drawing nearer.

In a panic, I took a step closer to the water's edge, urging her along. "We don't have time for references. We need to *move* because the storm is coming in fast, and we don't want to get washed away."

"It seems a little odd you are out here with nothing to do. It doesn't interfere with your schedule to do this?" Not budging even an inch, her gaze wafts down toward the footsteps pounding on the docks. It's clear to me now that the pirates are weaving up and down each row, thoroughly searching each boat, which seemed to slow them down a little, but it wouldn't take long for them to be here. "Do you hear that noise?" She cocked a brow in that direction.

"No, I don't hear anything, and besides it's probably nothing." A scowl started to cross my face before I remembered I was playing a role. "Ah, yes, as far as my schedule goes. I've docked my boat against the incoming storm, but I've navigated worse waters than this. If your ship is secured, we shall be fine. Why don't you show me to your boat, and we can look."

Her gaze turned skeptical, and I feared she was going to pass on my offer. To make the situation credible, I threw out a number to her in offer. "My normal rate is two thousand."

"Oh, yes of course." Her lips took a curious angle, like she was going to inquire further. By now the footsteps pounded toward us like galloping horses, pausing at the boat just a few feet from us. When they find nothing there, they'll turn this way, and it's too close for comfort.

*I didn't have time for an interview!*

"Look!" I blurted out, if you want to hire me, we gotta leave before they close the docks because it's going to get gnarly. Normally, I'd give you a list of references, and we'd sign a contract, but we don't have time with this weather."

Her head startled back, and she was quiet for a moment—way too long. I held my breath, dying a little each second, as I wished I hadn't been so curt. She swiped away the last of her tears with her sleeve, and eagerly breezed out, "Well, why don't I give you a tour of my boat and we can chat a little about the job." Turning on her heel, leading me further down the dock to a large yacht, she hitched her hands to the ladder and climbed it.

I skittered up behind her, tossing glances over my shoulder every other step. Boy, did I want to push her to make her go faster, but I was smart enough to know that wasn't going to win me this job. Instead, I shoved my hands in my pockets, and did my best to swallow my anxiety. When my feet landed on the deck, my stomach dropped what felt like a foot, in sheer relief. Gulping down the fear that had bubbled into my throat, I didn't think it was a good idea to tell her I'd never actually piloted a boat this big. I mean, I was sure it was a minor detail she didn't need to know, and it would be like riding a bike.

She headed to starboard, calling back, "Follow me. I'll show you to the wheelhouse."

Thankful to have a place to hide out, I followed her inside, adopting my best captain's gait and elevated chin. "Yes, I'm going to need to make sure it's suitable." My eyes traced the two throttles and buttons, and high-tech computer screens, and my brain started to swell immediately. I was clearly going to have to Google some stuff. "Looks great." I shot her a toothy grin, not at all as reassuring as I had hoped. Then rushed to add, "As an added safety precaution, why don't you find a life jacket because these seas are rocky. I'd feel better if you wore one, at least until we are out of the rough waters of the bay." I tried to sound as professional and cautious as I could, while still praying in my head I was convincing her.

"I can find a life jacket." Her smile held a hesitation before she added, "If you're sure you're up to this trip, I'll head back and untie us, so we can get going."

Excitement flooded my veins as I realized that was a job offer. Not just any job offer, but one that would find me some treasure. I fought to keep my smile tame when I said, "I'll set about pulling in the anchor and we should be fine. You have nothing to worry about."

"After I untie us, I'll head down to change into some dry clothes, and I'll be back to see if you need anything after that." As she left, I was relieved of the pressure of running from the thugs, but now had a new pressure—one that had everything to do with not getting us killed.

Letting out a slow breath, I located the choke, pushing it down, and turned the key. Sweet mama, it worked! The engine roared to life, and she purred like a kitten. "I'm going to do this." I chanted to myself as I adjusted my settings. "I'm going to escape those thugs and get this treasure." Pulling the sealed plastic bag from my satchel, I retrieved the treasure map. Still dry and preserved, I rolled it out, trying to pin it flat as I found my coordinates and set the GPS. A joyful and mischievous laugh rolled out of my mouth. "This is too easy."

I slowly pulled away from the dock, holding my breath as I steered out to sea. Once I cleared the marina, I let out a sigh of relief and smirked as I ramped up my speed. Rubbing my hands in glee, I stared studying the map.

I had taken my gondola out a few days earlier, trying to find the island where the treasure markings were. Even though I had easily found my way, I suspected the map's scale had to be off. I had these waters memorized, and I didn't recall ever seeing a diamond shaped island anywhere near here. According to the map, the island was just to the west of the bay, but there was nothing but open sea there. I was hoping I only needed to travel out a little further. It was an odd map with everything perfectly plotted exactly as the sea laid it out, except for that stupid island.

There were also weird markings on the map, one which looked like half of a gold heart attached to a figure eight with writing below it:

*True treasure can only be found by two souls fated for eternity.*

Shaking my head in disgust because I was never good with riddles, I cringed through the clue before sliding my gaze back to the water. It was dark, but I could see white-capped waves, bouncing this yacht all over the bay. I checked the radar again, making sure we were set, when out of the corner of my eye, I saw Evie coming back. I quickly stashed the map back into the plastic bag, zipped it as fast as I could, and shoved it into my satchel. My eyes locked on hers when she approached, and I found my captain's persona and saluted.

# Three

## Evie

Holding back my unease, I forced a queasy smile as I passed through the door and clung to the wall for balance. Now wearing a comfortable athleisure pants and jacket set, I was breathing more deeply, but it wasn't helping my overall feeling of wellbeing. I was born with sea legs, but these waters were so turbulent it made the bottom of my stomach quiver. "Boy," I pushed a calm tone while I maintained a hand on the wall for balance. "Are you sure it's safe to be out?"

"Yes, it's safe." He waved his hand in a dismissive way. "The waves are being funneled right into the bay and don't have room to spread out, but once we get out of here, we can head west, and everything will smooth out."

I looked past him, pretending to scan the sea, hoping he wouldn't see the heartbreak on my face. With no idea how it got this bad, my life had clearly turned into one big disaster. Despite working my life away from the time I was a young child, going to every audition my parents dragged me to, and putting on all the smiles they asked of me, it wasn't enough.

*It was never enough.*

They always had a critique for me, and pushed me even harder. I went along with it, because all I wanted was to feel loved by them, and I had convinced myself that eventually, I'd make them proud. Never in a million years would I have wanted to steal my sister's thunder on her wedding day. No matter how I tried to explain it to them, they would take her side. She's the one who insisted I be in her bridal party, wearing that ugly dress. She'd had to have known the paparazzi would sneak in, and it's not like I could have hidden when I was in the front of the church. If I had done what I had wanted to do, I would have worn black and stood in the shadows in the back, allowing her the entire spotlight.

After all the years of performing for my parents, I had finally given up. There was no point. I would never make them proud. Now I was left with the haunting thoughts of having wasted my life trying to please people who couldn't be pleased. It was time I did something for me. I was starting over by leaving the city forever.

The night sky was blanketed in thick storm clouds, and I couldn't see much other than the waves crashing into the front of the boat, and a few distant lights behind us. An odd thought popped into my head. In my moment of anguish, I had overlooked some details. "So," I cleared my throat and continued, "I never mentioned where I wanted to go. I'm a bit curious where you're headed."

He motioned to the radar. "I plotted out a course that got us out of the storm's way, and once we get there, I can adjust it to wherever you'd like."

His smile was convincing, but there was something odd about him. I had thought it was strange to find a spare captain roaming around. The more I studied him, the more I realized my suspicions might be correct. "Um, you know," I started with my voice small, "I think maybe I overreacted. This storm isn't anything to mess around in, and maybe—" My voice trailed off because I could tell he wasn't listening. His jaw dramatically dropped like the hinge had broken all the way off, and he seemed frozen. "Casper. Is everything okay?"

"Ah, it's Jasper." He seemed to pant, eyes locked on the sea. "Actually, there's a slight irregularity with the course I set." He was a bit befuddled in his words, before the panicked inflections poured in and he screamed, "If you could kindly prepare to be shipwrecked!"

My eyes flew to the windshield, doubtful I'd even see anything.

*Pancakes with guacamole!*

A biblical sized tidal wave—giant as the tallest skyscraper—was heading our way! Grasping for the radio, I turbo dialed, trying to find the frequency for the coast guard, calling out, "Mayday, Mayday!" It was no use! We were out of time; the wave was rolling in like a collapsing house of cards, and we were clearly going to be on the bottom. Tears flooded my eyes, burning the sockets as fear surged through me.

Why did I trust this stranger to pilot my boat? I could have so easily waited until morning. Nobody even knows I left shore, and they won't have any idea how I was washed away. This was the worst idea ever. I thought my night had been bad before, but it could never get worse than this.

*This isn't how I was supposed to die!*

I hoisted myself onto a wood-paneled door, clinging to the edges with a death grip as it buoyed on the rippling waves. Gratitude flooded my heart. Not only did I live, but I found something to float on. Having no recollection of how I had come to find this door, I fought back tears as I frantically searched for something familiar in the dark night. Apparently, I was in the sea all alone.

"Evie!" a deep voice rasped from somewhere near me. Turning to follow it, I made out the shadow of a man swimming closer. "I'm so glad you're okay." Jasper's voice was breaking in-between pants for air. "I was looking all over for you." Now within arm's reach, he held out his hand. "Here, take my hand."

Sliding my hand into his, I squeezed it with everything I had while stuttering out, "I-I won't let go."

He offered a bemused smile while his eyes stayed locked with mine. "This isn't the movie *The Titanic*. We aren't drowning. Look—" He rotated my floating door one hundred eighty degrees to face the opposite direction. Now I stared at a beach.

Not a regular beach with brown sand, or even smooth white sand. This sand was so white, it almost seemed transparent, and sparkled under the light of the stars, which shouldn't be possible because it was dark out. The trees that rose from the sand resembled palms, but they also glistened blue and green under the starlit sky. I was about to ask where we were, but his voice provided the answer to my question. "We crashed right by an island, and it's shallow here. You can walk to shore."

"Island? There's no island in the bay," I muttered, but I was clearly staring at an island that was so vibrant with bright colors that seemed to seep into one another, as if painted by a divine hand, while a lone mountain waterfall glistened in the moonlight as if it was pouring out crystals.

I must have hit my head harder than I thought.

I rubbed the goose-egged sized bump on the back of my head, while hoping to stop my mounting dizziness as I slid off the door. My feet met a sandy bottom. I started to ask if I was dreaming, but the pain in my head was too strong to be fake. "Where am I?"

I continued to squeeze Jasper's hand as he guided me to shore. "Do you remember what happened?" Tracing my memories, it didn't take me long to find one that stung. My sister's mean words clung heavily around my heart like a winter cloak I couldn't take off.

*I hate you!*

Swallowing the sting in my throat, I pushed that way out of my mind and focused on something else. While I was running to the dock, I overheard some guys talking about the thief who got away with their treasure map. I had no idea who they were, but they gave me the creeps with the way they spoke. They ran in one direction, and they frightened me so, I took off the opposite way.

When I ran into Jasper on the docks he was acting suspiciously. I had wondered if maybe he was the guy with the treasure map. Being the creative type, my imagination was always running wild, and I daydreamed about running away and treasure hunting with this handsome stranger. Before I could talk myself out of it, I let him convince me to go out in this storm, but I hadn't for a moment believed he was going to help me. He was up to something, and I had a pretty good idea what that was. I had momentarily romanticized how it would feel to find some treasure, and perhaps stop a thief—all to prove my family was wrong about me.

Getting real, it was a *bad* idea, but it was too late to turn back now. I needed a plan. He might be dangerous. I wasn't going to let him see I was onto him, so I purposely acted naïve to see if I could get more information, "Uh, the last thing I remember is running away from my sister."

"You don't remember anything that happened after that?" His face tilted toward me, but it wasn't unfriendly. We were on dry land now, and I instinctively dug my numb toes into the sand, soaking up the stored heat.

Slowly, my feet dried off and a mild warmth flowed up through my body, aiding my temperature's recovery. I was hyper focused on my extremities, making sure I could feel each one, when Jasper's voice cut off my thoughts.

"Do you remember meeting me on the docks?" he pressed, his voice holding more urgency.

I studied his face. He was handsome, in a ruggedly mysterious way, with dark hair and complementary dark eyes. The way he looked back at me, with his eyes burning into mine, made me further suspect he was still hiding something.

*Maybe he really is dangerous?*

I wasn't sure what to say, because I wanted to get more information out of him before I confessed to what I did know. I surely didn't want him to suspect I knew who he was. I weighed my options on how to proceed, until I remembered a low budget film I had done in high school where the main character had amnesia. It seemed like a silly trope, but it ended up being the perfect tool for the main character to play dumb. Since I was going for clueless, I leaned on that role, "Oh, eggs and bacon!" I screamed out as my hand fled over my mouth. "I don't remember you, but I totally played this role in a movie once and I know who you are!"

"Err . . . the guy you—"

"Married!" I cut him off because I wanted to make my act as believable as I could. I rushed to explain everything to set him up. "I totally must have amnesia, and I forgot you are my husband!" In my effort to convince him, I grabbed his hand and gave it a hearty squeeze. "It's going to be okay because I was in a movie once with this *very* same plot, and I know exactly what to do to get my memory back."

"Err, what?" He glared at me like I had lost my marbles.

"It's okay." I squeezed his hand again, feeling him stiffen at my touch. This whole act would only work if I did everything I could to make him think I was a ditz who wholeheartedly believed this. "I'm going to get my memories back, and trust me, this all ends so amazingly well." To reassure him, I squeezed my face into a sweet smile, but inside I was dying more than a little.

He lowered his brow, and now it looked more like a creepy caterpillar sitting on his face. I learned in my acting classes that meant he needed some convincing, so I didn't hold back. "You must remind me of all of the amazing things we used to do together, like how we fell in love. It's going to be tough, but just when we think it's no use, I'm going to get a tiny glimpse of something that sparks a memory, and then they all come rushing back from there."

He took a step back, releasing the hold I had on him, and yelled, "Evie, are you nuts?"

"No!" I snapped back. I assumed it was going to be difficult to convince him I had amnesia, but I hadn't planned on it being this hard. I was not giving up and I shouted back, "I'm not nuts, but I have no memory. Remember? I have Am-ne-sia!" I stretched the word amnesia as if I was talking to a ninety-year-old-deaf person. "Plus—"

"You don't have amnesia!" He cut me off, sounding a bit disgusted. If I had to be honest, I found this assertive thing he had going on to be very attractive. He grabbed both of my hands. "Listen, Evie," he squared his face with mine. "We met on the docks, and you hired me to pilot your yacht—"

"Of course, we did!" I carried on my impromptu act. "I've always loved a good falling-for-the-boss plot. I can't believe I get to be part of one in real life." I flashed my eyes heavenward like I was full of the swoons and couldn't wait to remember the rest of our love story.

He let out a noise that sounded a tad animal-like. I'll admit it was a bit off-putting, but I totally understood how hard this must be for him—or maybe that was just his hangry sound? I reached out, brushing the back of my hand against his cheek, hoping my touch would be reassuring to him. "It's okay, babe. We don't need to hash out all the details now. This is the part of the plot where we settle into life as we now know it."

I'll admit the scowl he gave me wasn't what I had hoped for, but I didn't take it personally. "Come on." I motioned with my head toward further up the beach. "Let's go find someplace to rest for the night, and we can chat about it in the morning." I smiled sweetly at him, hoping he was convinced I had lost my memory.

"Rest?" He went stone faced. "We don't even know if this island is safe. I don't think we should fall asleep without securing a campsite."

"It's okay." I waved his concern away as I headed up the beach. "There's always a little cave we can claim back here next to the rocks and trees. To find it, we must walk true north."

"Are you insane!" His jaw dropped so low his mouth looked like a giant cave with toothy stalagmites.

Easing into the brush, I tiptoed over the now pebbled terrain, careful of my surroundings as I walked toward the glade of trees. There had to be something up with this island because just like in my recent movie, I found the cave exactly where I knew it would be. Even though, I had pretended it was going to be there, the fact I found a cave sent a trickle of goosebumps along my spine. That was too co-inky dinky for me to feel calm about, but I couldn't let him see my hesitation, or it would blow my cover. I pushed forward. "See!" I called back as I pulled aside a concealing branch. "Here's the cave and if we are lucky, it should already have a place for a campfire."

The screech he emitted was a little much. In Hollywood we called that overacting.

"It's fine, honey." I headed into the cave while still finessing him to trust me. I called back, "Everything is going to work out just fine." Only now,

I wasn't so convinced, as a chill ran through my body, warning me to stay alert.

# Four

## Jasper

"Casper, sweetie." Evie returned to the cave with a bushel of dried leaves in her arms, dropping them in the fire pit, not even hinting she was the least bit surprised at the events rolling out before us. I was beginning to think she was a magical genie because nothing was adding up. Although she was the one with a brain injury, I was pretty sure I'd gone bat-poop crazy.

"It's Jasper. Jasper Knight." I didn't even look her way because I was busy untying my satchel from around my waist, where I had managed to wrap it before the impact of the first wave. My stomach felt like it was in my throat as I opened the flap and unzipped it. Thankfully, my precious map was still safe. Tucking it back down to the bottom, not daring to let it out of my sight, I focused my attention back on her mumbling.

"Ah!" Clasping her hands in front of her, she let out a satisfied sigh. "I love the way that sounds. So, did I take your last name, or did I hyphenate?"

The frustration pounding in my brain was exploding, but I couldn't convince her that she was wrong about us. The more I tried to explain it, the more she threw plot lines at me. She was seriously cuckoo. I decided instead of arguing with her, the better plan would be to play along until we found our way off this island, and I could ditch her. "Um, you kept your name," I murmured, fighting the urge to argue again.

"Right." She nodded, like she recalled this memory *that didn't happen.* "Of course, my career. I wouldn't have wanted to mess with my celebrity brand."

Still unsure how far to take this, I finally managed to say, "Exactly that," while I distracted myself by piling up the branches in the pit. I wasn't even going to ask where we would find fire, but I sat down next to the pit, not doubting it would happen.

As if she was reading my mind, she took two sticks from the pile and started rubbing them together, gently blowing on them. She was clearly wasting her time, but it was pointless to reason with her. Just when I opened my mouth to tell her it was time to give up, a perfect stream of smoke piped up from the stick. I slammed my eyes so far in the back of my head that it hurt, but oddly I wasn't even surprised at this point.

"I learned how to do this for my movie." A pleasant smile grew on her face as she fed the fire leaves and branches until a good-sized flame grew. Then she sat back right next to me, crossing her legs in front of her like it was normal for us to sit so close. When her gaze slid over toward me, the reflection of the flame danced in her eyes.

I had noticed she was this stunning when I first saw her, but I started to feel a nervous unease sitting this close to her. I'm not anti-social, but she kept batting her lashes, as if she truly believed I was her husband. It sent a nervous flutter to my gut, and just when I couldn't handle it anymore, I jolted and stuttered, "A-Ah, let me look at that knot on your head."

She didn't resist when I scooted over and examined her head, running my fingers along her scalp. Even though the knot was huge, it wasn't cut or bleeding. "It looks mostly okay. Be sure to take it easy, especially if you get lightheaded."

She was quiet about my assessment. When I returned my gaze to her face, there was a peacefulness in her eyes that drew me in. "Tell me about us," she said in a dreamy voice. "What kinds of things did we like to do together?"

She seemed so hopeful, and I didn't have the heart to destroy her fairy-tale. Not today anyway, and I certainly didn't want her to go back into her crybaby mode, so I tried to come up with something. "Uh, normal stuff. You know, eating. Talking—"

She leaned closer, the reflection of the flames dancing in her irises. "Do we dance?"

"Um...." My voice squeaked, and a nervous sweat beaded my brow. I mean—not nervous—but from the heat of the fire. I wasn't cut out for this storytelling stuff. I had never been in any sort of a romantic pairing before. I wasn't a huge fan of dancing, but I would imagine if we had been a real couple, we would enjoy dancing together. "Yeah, we do like to dance," I lied, slapping another layer of sweat on my brow.

"I knew I would marry a man who loved to dance." Her eyes locked on me, and they shone with an endless spiral of sparkles, emitting so much undeserved affection. "When I was little, and first saw how Prince Charming held Cinderella so lovingly, I knew I wanted a man like that."

"Yeah," I muttered under my breath, trying to turn my attention to the fire. "I think you told me that story once."

She laughed a good-natured laugh that brightened up her whole face. "I'm sure more than once, right?"

Pulling my lips into a forced grin, I replied in my best even tone, "Many times."

"Ah..." her sigh was wistful, the kind you'd make when you were re-membering your most cherished memories. "So," she went on, "you said you are a ship captain?"

I started to agree but stopped. What would she say if I told her the truth about myself? How I was a nobody. How I had grown up alone—many times going days without food—and became a professional thief. How everyone feared me, and no one had ever loved me.

It seemed ironic now. I spent my life devoid of love, wondering what it would be like, and here I was, by accident, with this insane woman who had been so easily convinced she was totally in love with me. So much so that the way she looked at me made my insides twist in turmoil. She *believed* we were together. She wouldn't look at me like that if I told her the truth. "I am, yes, a captain."

She slid her arm around my back. Warm goosebumps dotted my arms, and she giggled as she leaned even closer. "Do you always feel so rigid when we cuddle?"

Clearing my throat, I did my best to relax. Hating myself for lying, I yelled in my head this was the only way to get through the night because she wouldn't believe me if I did tell her the truth. "I'm apprehensive about what we are going to do next."

"Oh—" Her mouth made a perfect round circle when she tacked on, "a rescue boat will come for us sometime tomorrow."

My lips formed an amused grin, and a small chuckle slipped out. As much as I wanted to tell her she was *ridiculous*, there was something weird about this island. I wanted to believe her, so I kept my lips sealed.

"I'm telling you, babe." She butted her chin to rest on my arm, nestling her face into me. "It's all going to work out. It always does." The sensation of her being so affectionate toward me caused my breath to hitch in my throat. I don't think I could have spoken if I had wanted to, I didn't even try. I glanced down at her at the exact moment she lifted her face to mine. We were so close; her soft breath tickled my cheek. Then in a voice, barely above a whisper, she said, "I bet you are the goat of husbands."

Snorting, I bit back more waves of laughter. That was not what I had been expecting her to say. As hilarious as it was, the word husband seemed to burn deep in my chest. Her eyes were cemented on mine like she was expecting a response. I couldn't lie with her being so close to me. I came up with the most honest answer that would fit. "I never expected I would ever be anyone's husband."

"Really?" She looked honestly shocked; maybe even hurt. "You didn't want to marry me?"

"Oh, no," I rushed to defend how that came out all wrong, and from instinct, I pulled her even closer. "I didn't mean it like that. I meant I never expected to be so lucky to find someone like you."

"Right." Her eyes refilled with the sparkles they had held before. "Isn't that how it's supposed to be? Like when you meet your person, you know it's different."

I sunk my teeth hard into my bottom lip. This whole conversation was tripping me out. She was a stranger I had met only a couple of hours ago. Now her eyes pierced mine like I was her whole world. I kept playing along, and whispered, "I think so."

If I hadn't known better, I swore disappointment flooded her eyes. Instead of asking a follow-up question like I had been sure she would, she lowered her gaze and got quiet.

Her jaw clenched, almost as though she was holding her breath. When it seemed she couldn't hold it anymore, her cheek twitched, and her breath flowed out of her chest. Obviously deep in thought, she seemed to be working through her own memories. I didn't want to interrupt her, but I wasn't shy about letting her catch me looking at her. Oddly, I wanted her to know I was here.

When I was finally convinced her words had fallen away forever, her eyes slid over to mine, and before I had a chance to offer her a reassuring smile, she asked, "So, where were we going tonight, before our boat crash?"

Now, I swiped my brow, buying a few seconds. How am I supposed to play along with this story? *I can't just make up memories for her.*

At the same time, I'd be a complete jerk to go back on my word now, and say we weren't married. *Just get through this one night and then you can ditch her.*

Tomorrow I'd have time to figure out how to get off this island. It wasn't far from the bay, and if anything, there had to be boats all around the place I'd be able to flag down once daylight came. I could help her get in touch with her family, who could explain there was no time lapse, and they could help her understand she wasn't married. It could all be laughed off, but in the meantime, what do I tell her about what we were doing on a boat in a storm?

I couldn't tell her I was running away from thugs, but I pondered if maybe I could tell her about the map...I mean, we had made it to the island without even trying, and I was going to hunt for the treasure tomorrow. She would be full of questions about it. It might be nice to have some help, but then she'd want to split it with me, and she already had tons of money, and that didn't seem fair. Reaching to my side, I patted my satchel, making sure it was still there. "We were um, trying to get away to have some time together."

"I love that," she cooed, leaning her head back on my shoulder again. "I love that even after marriage, we still put each other first."

Maybe it's how lies taste, but a sour coating crept into my mouth. I found myself rolling my tongue on the roof, trying to rid myself of its flavor. I was a thief, and proud of it, but I had never been a liar, and I didn't like the taste it left in my mouth. Not wanting to add any more lies to keep track of, I was done talking for the night. "What do you think?" I casually looked over at her but made sure to lean away, careful not to imply anything as I stretched out on the ground. "You must be exhausted? You should close your eyes to rest, and I'll keep watch for you. It's going to be a big day tomorrow."

Her eyes traced my face, and if I'd I ever wanted to be able to read someone's mind, it would have been now. There was a shyness that took over her gaze. "Sure." She followed my lead, spreading out next to me, our bodies lined up parallel. Perhaps she'd been expecting us to cuddle, and it would have made sense with the whole camping situation and all, if we had actually been married. Something about lying next to her felt like it was going too far. Before she made any suggestions, I rolled over on my side and stared out of the cave entrance, keeping my gaze far away from her.

*Afterall, I have boundaries! I might be pretending to be married, but there would be no spooning with a stranger!*

# Five

## Evie

I was sleeping when a faint rustling drew me from my sleep. Pulling one eye open into a slit, trepidation budded in my chest when I searched for the noise. The fire had waned into nothing more than glowing embers and smoky haze, but it was enough to make out the shadow of Jasper sitting up. Seeing the noise was only him, I calmed until I noticed he was holding out a tattered piece of paper and tilting it toward the light while seemingly deep in thought.

Just as I had suspected. He had the stolen treasure map!

I had guessed it had been in that satchel he'd been guarding all day. Men were always so weird about their possessions, but he had been hypervigilant. Especially since he had taken the care to save it from the shipwreck. Even though I now had my suspicions about him being the thief confirmed, I was unafraid.

There was something about this moment, being so close to him, and being able to study him when he had no idea, that felt sacred. Jasper was intriguing to me. He had his mysterious ways, yet he was obviously caring because he had gone out of his way to go along with my amnesia skit even though I could tell he was totally uncomfortable, and terrible at lying. The poor guy was nearly trembling when I leaned my chin on his arm. If he had wanted to hurt me, he would have done it by now, and he sure wouldn't have gone out of his way to find me after the boat crashed.

Those thugs I had seen on the docks were bad dudes. Everything, from the way they spoke of murder, and revenge, to how filthy gross they were. I felt it in my core just being near them, but Jasper didn't give off any dark vibes. Oddly, I had learned to trust him in this short time, but was still insanely curious as to how he got messed up with dudes like them.

He had to be so brave. I didn't believe for a minute he was a ship captain, but he had a life outside of stealing treasure maps. He was extremely handsome. I noticed it right away, but especially now that I got to see him this close. He did have a deep scar on his neck below his ear, but that didn't hurt his appearance. If anything, it made him more alluring. I wish I could ask him about it, but I don't want to offend him, and the shape was so odd, it didn't look like an accident.

*Who are you?* I mouthed without sound.

I don't know how much time passed while I studied Jasper before my eyes drifted again. A moment later, a soft touch on my cheek brushed away the hair that had fallen in front of my face. His touch was so tender, it sent a thrill of goosebumps right through me. The warmth of his body so near wafted off of him, and I held my breath, debating on whether I should open my eyes or not. My gut told me to keep them closed. It was clear when I was awake that Jasper wore some sort of a shield, but now that he'd assumed I was sleeping, he seemed to be truly concerned about me, taking watch through the night while I slept.

Time passed, and Jasper got up. I opened one eye to see him kindling the fire, and when that was done, he took several laps around the cave, pausing at the entrance to gaze out into the night. I drifted in and out of sleep, and

I was about to offer to take a turn at watch so he could rest when he made a scuffling noise. I assumed he had finally laid down because it got eerily quiet. I opened my eyes to check, and he was gone.

# Six

## Jasper

Not wanting to risk having to play four hundred questions with Evie about what I was doing tomorrow, I decided it was best to get a head start on the hunt tonight. If I was as lucky as we'd been thus far, I would find the treasure, claiming it all for myself. I rubbed my hands together excitedly as I walked away from the cave. The treasure will be all mine, and nobody will even know about it.

Then I'll return to find Evie, and we'll figure out how to get off this island and put this awkward marriage play behind us. She really was a sweet lady, and I feel terrible she hit her head and all, but I had zero interest in being anybody's husband—real or pretend.

I pulled myself together, but didn't take my satchel. If by chance I wasn't back by the time she woke up, I wanted to leave something to show her I was coming back, and that's all I had. I could easily say I was out looking for berries or something. Besides, I wouldn't be able to read the map in the dark anyway. At this point I had it memorized. The X was on the beach on the other side of the island, which according to the scale shouldn't be more than a quick walk. I wasn't going to think about how I had already determined the map scale was off.

The best path would be to hang along the water's edge so I wouldn't lose my sense of direction. If I didn't fall in a hole or something, it would be a super simple trail. As I strolled along, I marveled as the whole island seemed to be wrapped in a peaceful vibe emanating from the waves crashing against jagged rocks and the rustle of trees swaying in a never-ending perfect breeze. The air was heavy with the scent of wildflowers, while exotic birds sang harmonious melodies. That was odd, because on the mainland, birds didn't sing at night. It was just another ridiculous thing about this island. It was paradise.

When the cave was no longer in my sight, and the first daylight broke the sky, I stumbled across something—let's call it a clue—that made me doubt I had thought this plan out as thoroughly as possible—pirates!

And not just any pirates.

*The ones whose map I had stolen*!

They crowded around me, like pigeons on breadcrumbs. Before I had time to think, it was too late to run.

"You know what we want." The burliest one stepped forward, putting his hands around my neck. "Give it back now, and we'll let you go free."

My hands flew to his massive-superhuman hands on my neck. I tried to pry them loose, but they didn't budge. He retaliated against my feeble attempt at defense and pulled upward, until only the tips of my toes touched the ground. It was a bit of a compromising position which left me struggling to breathe, but he must not have known who he was messing with.

If he thought I was going to hand this map over after everything I went through this week, he was nuts. He may be an ugly pirate with bad breath, but I was one of the most successful thieves. I never gave back my loot. "I don't know what you're talking about," I managed to choke out.

"Sure, you don't. Maybe this will help you remember?" He squeezed his hands tighter around my throat, draining out all the air I had in my windpipe. Just when I thought my neck would snap, he slammed me back until I fell against a tree. Despite having the wind knocked out of me, I scampered to my feet, ready to scram. One of the dwarf pirates flew in—yes, I said that correctly, he *flew*. I didn't see wings but I'm sure that was the correct action verb—and jabbed a machete at my throat.

"He said, give him *his* map." When he popped the p on the word map, he jabbed the tip of his blade into my throat, and it broke through my skin. Clearly, this guy had a patience problem. The piercing stung worse than any knife fight I'd ever been in. When my life started to flash before my eyes, I knew it was over.

Not my life, but this hunt. It wasn't worth getting beheaded.

Though, it would have been epic to have that treasure.

Was it greedy to think, just once, I would have a chance to get ahead in life?

I didn't have time to answer because he furled his lips, and snarled out, "Give me the map!"

"Okay." I held up my hands, and opened my mouth as wide as I could. "I don't actually have it on me, it's—" My words halted so fast my tongue got whiplash. I couldn't tell him the map was back at the cave, because that's where Evie was, and I couldn't risk them finding her!"

He leaned his face closer, his eyes glued to my lips as he waited for me to speak. It was a bit of a scary predicament, but thankfully, I had gotten better at lying, and I blurted out, "It was on the boat when it crashed!"

"You're lying." His breath was hot on my face, and he moved in even closer. Though I was scared out of my mind, I had a fantastic distraction from the fear. He had so many foul odors coming from him, his odors had odors. I was fighting hard not to vomit back in his face.

"You don't need it anyway," I snapped back, rushing to come up with a new plan. "I memorized it, and I can tell you exactly where to go." I couldn't believe I didn't think of this sooner, but it was perfect because the treasure was buried on the other side of the island, which meant they could go that way, and I could run back to Evie to help her escape before they got to her.

His beady eyes narrowed, but they never left my face. The first pirate who had bullied me stepped forward again, and I understood the meaning of the phrase "if looks could kill." Thankfully, they couldn't, and I was still alive.

For now.

"It's, ah, on the other side of the island. Remember the island is diamond shaped." I pointed to the water's edge. "Follow this path and when you get to the point on the other end, dig."

I didn't know if I was expecting him to let me run free immediately after I gave up my information—I mean, it would have been nice—but that's not how it went. Instead, he breathed on me for a while longer, and again he went with the machete—this time jamming it into my back. "Did you think we'd let you go?" He poked the tip of the weapon hard, breaking flesh again, forcing me to walk forward.

These pirates were so testy.

As I moved forward, leading them on the path I had planned for myself, a strange emotion washed over me. Instead of being scared for myself, or upset that I lost the treasure, I felt relieved I was able to lead them away from Evie.

What did that mean?

# Seven

## EVIE

Night had fallen and there was still no sign of Jasper. I had left the cave earlier and gone down by the water to wash and look for wreckage debris that might have floated in. I wasn't lucky though. The things I found were pieces of the boat I couldn't identify, and they certainly weren't useful. Starved, and thirsty, I knew not to drink the saltwater. Instead, I collected coconuts and brought them back to the cave, but I didn't have a way to open them. I hoped Jasper would figure that part out when he got back. I supposed I should have been mad he'd ditched me, but I had this unsettled feeling in my gut that even though he had willingly left, something was wrong, and he hadn't planned on being gone all day.

The main reason I believed that was because he had left his man purse here. He had guarded that thing as if it was gold all day yesterday, even sleeping with it. I had a hard time believing he had left me for good, or he would have taken his bag. I wished life had real background music like the movies did, so I would at least understand how I was supposed to be feeling right now.

The sun had departed, leaving me chilled, and I made my way to the stone pit and set about starting the fire again. Earlier I had made several trips for branches, and I had quite the collection, but this time the sparks didn't come as easily. The branches didn't feel as dried, or tough, but they definitely seemed more stubborn. I rubbed them fast, I rubbed them slow, I even tried different angles, but nothing worked. I was shivering now in the dark, alone.

A sinking feeling settled into my gut, and for the first time since we crashed, I was scared I might die.

I shouldn't have, but I let my mind wander, thinking about how no one came looking for us today. I never saw one boat, or even a plane overhead. This island was completely deserted. Although I'd found coconuts, I still didn't have a way to open them. Then the worst thought of all...

What if Jasper doesn't come back?

*I could seriously die here all alone.*

That scene was never in any of my movies.

In my jitteriness, my sticks dropped from my hands, as if they couldn't take the directions my brain was giving them. Instead, they were listening to my shrinking heart. It was so full all day, and I had kept my spirits up, but now these nagging thoughts were taking hold of me, leaving a burn in the back of my throat despite how cold it was. My eyes welled up with tears, and even though no one was here to see me, I fought them back because to me, they were a sign of defeat.

I wasn't going to cry about this!

Crying didn't help anything, and it certainly wouldn't get me off this stupid island. The tears didn't listen, and they budded up in both my eyes, swelling to the point where that's all I could see. Swiping my hand at my eyes, I cleared them away. New ones came faster, and before I could wipe them, they fell.

Stupid tears!

Now I was mad. Crying, I called out in frustration, "No one is coming to save me, and if that's the case, then I'll have to save myself." I got up from the ground with new determination, ready to find a way off this island, and made my way to Jasper's bag. I didn't feel even a little bad as I rummaged through it. My fingers dug right to the bottom, and my lips curled into a pleased grin when I found it—the map.

I was born at night, but not *last* night.

Jasper *was* the thief who had stolen a treasure map and now he was missing. There was a real chance he was in trouble. I had a choice. I could get off this island and leave him behind, or I could go after him and maybe find a treasure too...

A thrill spiraled though my body, as I selected my path. Strapping the satchel across my body, I stuffed the map back inside and set off to find Jasper.

I took deep breaths as I hiked along the water's edge until I quickly identified a fresh set of tracks in the sand. They had to be Jasper's, and I stayed right on them. The air was humid and thick, as if it alone could nourish the tropical plants all around me. The full moon shone from its perch in the sky, giving me just enough light to guide me. I was careful to scan behind all the nearby trees and practiced being light on my toes. I shouldn't be going farther onto this island by myself, but the tracks I was following compelled me to see where they went. Moving cautiously, I advanced, I could hear the faint sound of voices.

Not just any voice, but Jasper's voice.

"Evie!"

I craned my neck forward until I spotted Jasper tied to a tree. All the trees in my peripheral vision were tall palm trees, but this one was random and out of place with its dark gnarled branches, casting eerie shadows on the beach sand. It was almost as if the tree was put here for the sole purpose of creeping me out. I swallowed my chills, chalking it up to just another weird thing about this island.

Swooping into his side, I immediately went to work untying the ropes, and I didn't stop until I had Jasper's arms freed. He flew forward, wrapping his arms around me, squeezing me tight. His shoulders quivered as he rasped out, "Are you okay?"

"Yeah, I'm fine," I squeaked out, my morning fears of dying alone on this island melted.

As if a switch went off, his shoulders stiffened, and he backed out of our embrace. His chest fell more with each breath as he stood, staring wide-eyed and speechless. I was about to ask what had happened, but the spiral in his eyes made my heart ramp up. His gaze bounced from my eyes to my lips and back to my eyes before he blurted out, "I'm sorry I left you. I was so stupid and fixated on something so dumb, that I missed seeing what was right in front of me."

Still a little clueless, I didn't reply because I wanted to hear more, and he didn't disappoint as he went on, "I'm also sorry I've been lying to you. It's not right. I was trying to avoid a bigger argument, but I made things worse."

"W-What are you lying about?" My gaze darted to the side, and I kicked at the sand, already knowing what was coming.

"I lied to you when I agreed that we were married. We aren't. I'm not your husband...or even your boyfriend."

I smirked as he confessed my lies, "I misled you for many reasons. I'm also not a ship captain. I'm sort of a-ah, well, it doesn't matter." He stuttered as he raked his hand through his hair. I found it endearing how flustered he got when he went on, "But what matters is you know something weird happened to me. This sounds crazy, but I feel like something special brought us here."

I smiled at him coyly. "I'm the one with the head injury, but even I know it was a boat that brought us here. It wasn't that special."

"Okay, I'm going to try one more time to tell you the truth, so my conscience is clear." His eyes traced my face, and when I didn't say anything he went on, "I offered to be your captain because I wanted to hunt for treasure, and I had this map—this real treasure map I stole from pirates—and I was using it as a guide when we crashed into this island. Last night, I snuck out to find the treasure, but the pirates found me first. They forced me to take them to the treasure. When we found the spot, we dug in the sand and found a box."

Pulling my hair over my shoulder, I smoothed it a few times as he confirmed everything I had already guessed. "Okay," I replied softly and decided to give in too. "Ah, while we are at it," I rushed, "I might have lied about the amnesia. I don't have any memory loss. I actually saw the pirates on the dock. When I found you, I thought it would be fun to go on a treasure hunt, so I made all that up to try to get you to confess."

"You what?" His lips spread into a grin that was so sensational, it made the corners of his eyes crease, and he laughed, a deep bellied laugh like he thought I was the funniest person in the world. I hadn't planned on it being a joke, but I joined in his laughter. It was like, for the moment, we both forgot we were still stranded on this stupid island with no way home, and we giggled together, finding home in each other.

When the laughter faded, he swapped his humorous expression for a more serious mask and in a low voice he said, "The pirates tied me up, and then tried to open the box, but it wouldn't open, and something happened to them. It was like they went insane, or got scared, and they all ran back to their boat, leaving the box behind." He pivoted on his heel and motioned to the wooden box by the tree. He ushered me closer, and we both reached forward in unison, gently touching the box . . .

The lid opened right up, almost as if it was spring loaded.

My eyes widened as I glanced back at Jasper, and I held my breath as we both slowly peered inside. I don't know what I was expecting to find, but it was a ratty old note. I lifted the note, keeping one eye on him, knowing this note had to have come from somewhere. If he was making up this pirate story, it wouldn't explain how he had this box, or this piece of paper that hadn't been soaked and ruined in the ship wreckage.

As I slowly unfolded the tattered parchment—darkened with age and branded with the same weird figure eight sign that was on the treasure map when I noticed when I looked in his satchel—I was overcome with a tingling sensation, starting in the tips of my fingers and spiraling down to my toes. It was pulling out all my doubts, all of my worries, and fears and pushing in new hopes and dreams into the voids that were left.

My heart pounding against my rib cage, as I scanned the faded ink calligraphy. I had a glittering perception when I read:

*This anointed quest is for the chosen one,*
*You can't return until it's done.*
*Finding your secret identity is just the first part.*
*Your mission isn't done until you open your heart.*
*Only soulmates can unlock this island,*

*The reward of wealth is each other's hand.*

My eyes lifted, regarding Jasper, and he was peering in the box. As I followed his gaze, I saw what he was looking at. Inside the box was a small mirror, just big enough to reflect both of our faces.

"What is this?" I lowered my hands, still clenching the note.

"I don't know what it is." He stepped closer to the box, half-buried in the translucent sand. "When you read it, something inside me changed. I saw a giant figure eight wrap around a heart."

"Hmm." I mulled, still perplexed by the whole thing. I shrugged off his comment to another weird thing about this island, when something above stole our attention. A comet blasted through the sky, headed straight to the sea. As it glittered down, it slowed, and right before it hit the surface, it rolled into a ball of light. With a flash, the sky lit up and right where the comet had been, was a ship heading in our direction.

"That must be our ride home!" I exclaimed, jerking my hand to the ship, only half believing what I had just seen. Excitement burst through my entire body, and I jumped up and down, ready to race toward it.

"Right..." Jasper's brow lowered, but he tacked on a grin as he added in a curious tone, "Or more pirates."

I knew better than to be negative. That ship was meant for us. I took his hand, ready to propel him forward, but quickly paused. Something about it made me feel like he was holding my heart. I couldn't explain what had happened any more than he could, but I also couldn't deny something had intervened. Slowly I laced my fingers into his, giving him a reassuring squeeze. "I think we're going to be okay. Even though we sailed in a ship, I believe it was fate that brought us here."

"Yeah, that's what scares me a little." Jasper took a few even steps toward the ship. "I'm wondering what *else* fate has in store for us." He stared forward at the boat that was now tendering offshore. "But I think we are about to find out..."

# Eight

# Jasper

Throwing my arm out protectively in front of Evie, I rasped, "Don't move." An unfamiliar crossbones emblem flashed from the side of the large boat that didn't hint at it being the coast guard. A shirtless man with a peg leg roamed the deck in black and white ragged striped pants, and the sun gleamed off the blade of a large knife sheathed at his waist. I wasn't going to be a sitting duck while we watched that boat dock. They probably had men in the back loading a cannon as we spoke. Dying on this beach—while Evie bawled over my dead body—was not going to be *my story*.

"It's a boat, and there are people on there!" She pointed in excitement as she pushed on my arm, trying to get past me. "They might have food and can give us a ride."

Yesterday, I wouldn't have cared a lick about Evie. I'd shake and bake out of here, leaving her to figure it out on her own. I might even have felt relieved to have someone decoy them while I escaped. Today, my heart twisted, begging her to see the danger. We only had a minute window to get ahead of peg leg and his friends. I grabbed her wrist and yanked her back toward the brush. "It's more pirates. They might be more of the same, or a completely different group, but either way, we've got to run."

Catching her off-guard, she stumbled forward, but caught herself, and allowed me to pull her. Her eyes were wide, and she didn't utter a word as I propelled us back to take cover. I had a pretty good idea of the layout of this small island. There wasn't any place to hide, and nowhere to get off. The best plan was to keep moving, staying one step ahead of them until they gave up...or worst-case scenario caught up to us.

She pulled to the east, back toward the beach that led to the cave, and I growled, "No, we can't go back that way. We'd get surrounded." I tugged her arm, spinning her to the west, revealing uncharted muddy water nearly buried in mossy trees and thick grass. "This way."

She planted her feet, jerking her body to a stop. "It's a swamp." Her eyes begged for clarification.

I cut a glance back to the boat, finding it already anchored, and they were dropping a small dingy down into the water. I swallowed, gambling on any gators being a better choice. "We don't have time to talk this out. We must get ahead of them. We do that by going where they'd least expect first." I pulled her forward with even more urgency. "Move!"

"I'm not really that fond of cardio," she huffed out but stayed on my tail as I propelled her through the ankle-deep waters until they became knee high, and eventually waist level. At which point, I decided it was time to make our way to land. I turned in a circle, unsure of which shore would be safest. The north shore was barren and desert- like, with few places to hide. The south shore was thick with tropical trees and brush, which would provide plenty of places to hide, and likely some food for us, but I wasn't sure what *else* was hiding in the brush.

Likely there'd be spiders at the very least.

At the very worst...I swallow, not wanting to entertain that thought.

My eyes tracked from north to south, and I steered Evie to the south. My gut said we don't want to be sitting ducks in the desert. "Get your leg, and your peg and come on shore," I joked as I assisted Evie out of the water. We were both weighed down with heavy, wet clothes, shivering, starving, and exhausted. I scratched my head and studied the immediate area, completely overgrown without a fresh footprint in sight.

It appeared relatively safe.

We had trudged for hours, and if the pirates did what I assumed they would, and went in the opposite direction, we'd have a few hours to stop. As much as I hated to stop, I had to get real. We needed to stay hydrated and rested. "Let's clear some area behind this first row of trees. We'll be hidden but can keep our eyes on the water. It will give us time to dry off, take turns napping, and find something to eat before we go out on land."

Evie heaved an exhausted breath. "Sounds good to me."

"I know it's not comfortable but try to keep as much mud on you as you can to stay camouflaged."

While giving herself an officious once over, she scoffed. "I don't think that's going to be an issue."

We moved forward into the jungle. I pulled the lowest branches back carefully, so they didn't break, or shake the leaves off, as I didn't want to leave any clues where we'd been. While pointing to the ground, I cautioned, "Try not to step in the mud as it leaves prints. Step on the rocks, branches, and leaves."

"What do you think is back here?" Evie whispered, crouching her body as small as possible.

"I purposely tried not to think about that." I lifted another low branch for her to duck under, and then pointed behind a large tree trunk. "If we tuck up against this tree, the branch will camouflage us. Until I have a chance to explore a little, I'm not comfortable going any deeper in."

She plopped down, ungracefully, landing on her side, grunting out several heavy breaths as her eyelids became hooded. "Please don't tell me they don't have room service here, because I'm exhausted and starving."

My gaze traced her body. Aside from the fact she looked like she'd been rolling with the pigs, she'd gotten several large scratches on her arm. It didn't surprise me to see her so banged up, but other than her constant sarcastic coping remarks, she hadn't complained once. For an alleged spoiled movie star, she handled the near ambush well. She certainly was tenacious. "Since you're already laying down, why don't you take the first nap. I'll keep an eye out while trying to find some berries or something we can eat."

When she didn't reply, I assumed she was already nodding off, and took that as my cue to go bring home the bacon—literally. I can't even imagine the kinds of wild pigs that would live out here... We needed something smaller, hopefully already dead.

A squirrel or bird perhaps.

I stepped away from Evie while keeping my stance low to the ground. It was so eerily quiet, the hairs on the back of my neck rose, giving me the suspicion that I was being watched.

I froze.

Pivoting around at the slowest speed, I checked as far back as I could see in every direction. Trees, roots, vines, and tall grasses that didn't look like they'd ever been stepped on. I scanned high and low, and nothing caught my eye. I risked another step as my heart literally quaked inside my chest. Never in a million years would I have thought I'd be doing something like this, but with Evie counting on me, I didn't want to disappoint her. I had to keep her safe and taken care of.

I repeated my scan high and low, and still nothing, so I took another three steps, passing a huge tree that I felt compelled to duck behind. "Phew." I panted. It was muggy and hot, and now that we weren't in the water, the humidity hung heavy in my lungs. My eyelids grew heavier with exhaustion. Before I talked myself out of it, I found myself sliding down the tree trunk to sit.

*I just need to rest for a few minutes to think.*

A deep yawn spiraled from inside my lungs, pulling my mouth wide open, as I struggled to keep my eyes open so much they watered.

*I'm exhausted.*

My eyelids drooped even more. It was so amazing to give my eyes a break.

My breathing evened, and my shoulders relaxed as my head fell back against the thick tree stump, and I was drifting into a peaceful—

Zzzzzzz.

# Nine

## Evie

Sniffing at the light tickle on my nose, I tried to wrinkle it away to continue my slumber. Rest was blissful, as every tendon in my body had been stretched beyond what I presumed possible. My ankles puffed from the miles of trudging, and my back throbbed out its own heartbeat of pain. Add the pure exhaustion, I had no plans to wake up any time soon.

Like a cat trying to nuzzle at my nose in a sweet Eskimo kiss, the tickling continued. I giggled, as it set my dreams to respond. Now I was seeing my favorite childhood cat, Princess Flufferson. She'd left this earth years ago, but lived in my dreams, where she was always warm and snuggly. I leaned into the softness, pining for a deeper caress.

*Oh sweet, Princess Flufferson …*

I sighed, missing her essence so much, I grew nostalgic remembering her white puff ball head.

*Hissssss.*

My eyes sprang open.

A neon-snot-colored snake hissed directly into my eyes! His elongated form spiraled around the branch above me, and he flicked out his black forked tongue, narrowly missing the tip of my nose.

Sucking back a giant gasp, I flattened my body against the tree, trying not to make any sudden movements. *"Jasper..."* I whispered through clenched teeth, unable to create any more space. I shifted my gaze to both sides, but other than trees and vines, my peripheral vision was clear, Jasper was likely still gathering food, which meant I was stuck here alone.

Not alone.

*Alone would be better than this!*

I shifted my legs but returned them straight out when I discovered there was no way I could stand up with this serpent hanging directly above me. My best bet was to quickly—and ever so smoothly—shimmy to the side to get out from underneath it, and then bolt.

Where I would go wasn't a question I could answer. If I ran south, I hit the swamp. I also didn't know what direction Jasper was hunting, and I didn't want to wander too far off from base, because everything looked the same. There wasn't a way for me to mark my way back . . . I scanned the horizon, planning.

*Hissss*

Goosebumps spiraled all over my body, giving me the total creeps. *Out came his tongue, so pointy and long, and I was gone!* My leg jutted out as far as I could spread it, and I rolled out of his way, and scrambled to my feet, not taking the time to even figure out what direction I was running. I was smart though. I counted my steps. Fifty. Then I halted right next to another tree and vine. Yes, I doubled-checked that vine to make sure it was in fact a vine and not another snot snake.

As I rested my hands on my knees, I caught my breath and looked back the way I came. No snake following me. I must be safe. As a precaution, I cut a glance in the opposite direction. More trees and more vines, but no snake.

My gaze fell back behind me.

Or did I come from that direction?

Nah, I wagged my head, my brow furrowing. That way just had trees and grass and vines, and the other direction had...trees and grass and vines...

*Oh no!*

My bottom lip quivered as I turned in a circle, getting myself even further mixed up. I had no idea which direction I had come, which meant, I had no idea how to get back. But I knew my steps, and fifty steps weren't a lot.

Right?

I could pick a direction, run fifty steps, and if that wasn't the right direction, I'd come back and use this as my new base. I chewed the side of my cheek, my anxiety peaked. I'd needed to find a way to mark my trail, or I was going to continue to get deeper into the brush with no way back. I didn't have anything on me, but quickly came up with the idea to break a vine and tie it around a branch like a flag. It couldn't be too obvious, though, or it might give me away. It must be a low branch that's camouflaged, and only I know how to check it. I nodded, liking my plan.

It had to work.

# Ten

## Jasper

"Uuuaaaaahhhhhhh." I yawned awake while scratching my stomach. Several unrecognizable bug bites had formed tiny hills on my flesh, and the itch was hard to ignore.

But even with the bug bites, my nap hit the spot. My eyes peeled open slowly, one at a time. Never alarmed when I woke in unfamiliar scenery because I was used to sleeping outside and in random places, it took my brain an extra second to register the jungle. Jolting, I checked both my sides and with no sight of Evie, I jumped to my feet. My memory flooded back.

I left her napping by the swamp shore!

*I'm sure she's fine.*

I forced a calm breath and stretched lightly over my head. No need to panic. She's more than likely getting her much-needed rest . . .

*Unless Peg Leg caught up to her!*

*Okay, panic!*

*I should have known better than to leave her.*

I turned in a full circle, assessing my surroundings. Thankfully, I was resourceful enough from living outside all these years to be able to gauge directions with the position of the sun. I combined that with my memory of the twisted knot patterns of the trees and waded my way back through the tall grass the way I had come. The grass was thick and so healthy, it wasn't immediately obvious someone had traipsed through it. That was more reassuring to me than worrisome, as covering our tracks was my highest priority.

I got lucky and picked a direct path, making it back to base in less than five minutes. To my surprise, Evie wasn't napping anymore.

No need to immediately sound an alarm.

First, I checked around the surrounding trees, and when nothing turned up, my heart slammed against my ribcage, and twisted, pumping fear through all my extremities.

Normally, I'd never shout to announce my whereabouts, but I was savage, and can handle my own. Evie couldn't and I feared for her safety. I didn't care if I risked my own life. "Evie!" I called, low at first, hopeful she'd gone only a few feet out of my sight. I waited, listening to my echo, but when I didn't get a return call, I yelled louder, "Evie!"

Nothing.

Sweat frosted my lower back, both from the humidity and all-consuming horror. Evie's smart, and she wouldn't have wandered off, which meant...she had been taken captive. She's too sweet and naïve to make it out of any captivity alive. She's going to need rescuing if it's not already too late.

*How do I find her?*

*My stomach did a triple-double flip. How could I be so dumb to leave her alone with pirates roaming around?*

*Am I really that stupid?*

My eyes dropped to the ground, covered in tall grass almost up to my waist at some points. It might have been my imagination, but I could make out a narrow trail that some*thing* passed through recently. I didn't have any proof that it was Evie, but out of other clues and against my better judgement, I stepped and paused, calling softy, "Evie."

Nothing. I step a few more times, calling a little louder, "Evie!"

*Snap!*

Startling I jumped back as my gaze fell to the ground, and a sigh of relief tumbled from my lips. *It's just a twig—*

*A twig that's attached to a string!*

A giant net dropped from the sky.

Stuck in slow motion, I froze, unable to run! Apparently, I tripped on a snare trap, and it wrapped me up in one felled swoop. I was both lifted off the ground, flipped upside down, and hanging like a bat from a branch.

There was no way out, and even if there was, it's a loooong way down.

*Gulping, I set my mind on the positive. Good thing I'm not scared of heights.*

# Eleven

Eleven, twelve, thirteen steps, and—

"Evie!" Jasper's muffled voice echoed from somewhere.

I checked in all directions and called back, "Jasper."

"Up here!"

Arching my neck, I nearly shrieked when I saw the size of the net dangling above my head. I immediately gasped and skirted to the side to take cover. I'd been in this movie before, too! There's always another net next to the first, and I wasn't going to wait around for it to scoop me up.

"Evie!" Jasper's voice grew more desperate.

"I'm still here," I called out, while peeping around the tree I cowered behind. "I had to get out of the way before I got scooped up, too."

"You must get me down before those pirates come back and find me trapped in their net. They couldn't be far, which means it won't be long."

"Oh yes." I scanned the area, looking for something to assist my mission, but nothing popped out. "In the movie, the hero climbed up his body and cut the rope with the knife he had in his boot. I don't suppose you have a knife in your boot, do you?"

"If I had one, do you think I'd still be hanging here?" Jasper's exhausted voice responded.

"Right?" I scratched my head, as this was a real conundrum. "Well, I have seen it play out in the more unrealistic movies that some cheeky monkey can come out to help untie you, but I'm guessing that's not going to happen, either—"

"—Evie, you're wasting time! *You* need to climb the tree and untie me. It's not that hard."

"Oh." My eyes did a once over the massive tree with prickly looking needles jutting out of the branches. "I *could*, but did you see how tall it is?"

"Of course, I saw how tall it is!" Jasper was loud, almost imperious. "I'm hanging upside down from it, Evie, please."

"Of course." My voice was a little woeful, as I needed to work on my bravery inflections, but I was still awfully exhausted. Careful not to trigger another snare trap, I selected my steps methodically. I'd never climbed a tree this size before, and I wasn't quite sure I had the arm span to reach all the limbs, especially the first one. It would be nice to have something to stand on to give me a boost.

Straining my eyes to search the terrain as far back as I could in all directions, I found nothing and resigned to the fact that I'd have to use my strength, and a good old-fashioned running start. I backed up several steps, making sure my path was clear. When I was a good ten steps back, I crouched down, and took off at top speed. Just when I was below the branch, I lifted one foot for a layup, reaching my arms high over my head, and I was swallowed up by a net and flung upside down. It was so slick it felt like a carnival ride, and I barely squealed. "Well," I called out after I confirmed with my eyes what I knew had happened, and the ground was a looong way below me. "I don't think that plan worked."

"Sure didn't." Jasper growled. "Why don't you just use the knife in your boot to cut yourself free?"

"Funny." I half laughed, as dread started to sink in. Up until this point, I was doing everything I could to pretend I was on a movie set and none of this was real. Now that I was hanging upside down in a tree, with no escape...reality was hitting me hard. "Jasper," my voice weakened. "I don't want to die."

"Me either," he grumbled.

"That's not your line," I teased back, trying to take my mind off our impending doom. "You're the hero. You're supposed to say, 'Evie, don't worry, I'll save you!' And you're supposed to rasp it out, and not sound like such a weenie."

I thought he'd laugh, but I could understand how he wouldn't consider this a laughing situation. However, he did surprise me. In a firm voice, laced with empathy, he affirmed, "Evie, I'm not giving up. I'll try to save you."

# Twelve

## Jasper

We hung for hours, the blood pooling in the crown of my head created so much pressure it felt as if my forehead would burst. That, combined with the lack of food, dehydration, and exhaustion took its toll, and I drifted in and out of consciousness. At some point, someone tugged on the line, but I was so out of it, not only did I have no fight in me to escape, but I had no real awareness of where I was anymore.

Shadows came and danced around me. Some resembled trees, and some might have been pirates. I also thought I saw some cheeky monkeys, but they were more likely in my dreams. One thing was certain, Evie's voice never left me. That might have been a hallucination as well, but she talked me through each moment. "Jasper, we're going to be okay. Jasper, I really don't think this is that bad. Jasper, in the movie, the hero had gold to pay off the pirates. Do you have gold?"

That one made me smirk.

Or at least I wanted to smile.

I didn't have the capacity to move my lips anymore, and I was starting to be okay with the idea of going to sleep for good. I never wanted to die before, as I didn't feel like I ever had a chance to live, but at this point, it seemed like it would be peaceful. Better than waking up again to experience the kind of death those pirates wanted to give us.

Time passed, and I had no idea how long I slept. At some point, my ability to zone out reality became impossible, as my aching body throbbed harder and my insatiable hunger and thirst roared to life, jolting my eyes wide open.

Darkness.

Bone chilling damp air.

Were we back in the cave?

My hopes were immediately deflated as my hands found the floor underneath me. Unfinished wood I didn't dare run my fingers along as it was so rough, it would surely fill my palm with splitters.

"Jasper." Evie's sweet voice called softly, pulling my face to turn the other way. As I waited for my eyes to adjust to the absence of light, relief flooded my body.

*She was alive.*

"Evie." My whisper burned my hardened throat, but I was desperate to hear her voice more. "Are you okay?"

"I'm better now that you're awake." She must have been lying right next to me, because her tender hand found mine before my eyes un-fogged. A warm inhale came in like a hiccup, and I squeezed her hand so tightly, as if holding hands had the power to save us.

So many questions looped through my mind, but I still didn't know if it was safe to talk, and I whispered, "Do you know where we are?"

"On their boat in a jail cell," her voice was quiet, but not secretive. "We went down a flight of stairs and a long hall, so I'm guessing in the back of the boat."

A lump formed in my throat. That's the last place I wanted to be. "How bad is it?"

"It's mostly okay, for jail. The reason why you can't see anything is because it's night. During the day, there's a small amount of light which comes through a window."

Anxiety thumped to my heart, ramping it up. Evie had been surviving this whole time without me. My guts twisted when I imagined how frightened she must have been. I can't believe I was passed out this whole time, and they didn't just kill me to get rid of me. What is their reason for even bothering to keep us alive?

A small round window was at the very top of our cell, far out of reach for me. Now that my eyes had adjusted more, I could register a narrow beam of moon light. It cast a sliver of brightness so small, but it gave my eyes enough contrast to see the shadows, and I started to make out shapes. Evie's form finally came into focus. "How long have we been here?"

"Just one night and day. They gave me a little food and water twice a day. One time you woke a little—or at least I thought you were awake, because you were making a lot of gurgling noises—and I got you to take a few sips of water. I think that's the only reason you made it. You were really putting on a show for a while."

I squeezed her hand again, grateful to have an ally, as I'd never really had one. I'd always done life alone. Tiny shivers quaked through her hand, revealing how cold she was. With it being frigid temps, so was I. I was compelled to hold her closer, and I dropped her hand, extending my arm out, inviting her closer. "I don't mean to make you uncomfortable," I explained. "You're shivering, and I thought maybe if we held each other, we'd both warm up."

At first, her gaze fell on me with a straight lipped stare, but she slid over and laid her head on my chest. I wrapped my arm around her, pulling her into a tight bear hug. "Does it get warmer in here?" I breathed into the air, surprised I couldn't see my breath.

"A little during the day, but I wouldn't say it's comfortable." Her breaths were even against my chest, shudders seemly lessoning with each one.

"Did they say why they are bothering to keep us alive?" My voice cracked, as it hurt so badly to force anything out my throat, dried up like clay.

"No."

I waited for her to tell me what happened in the movie, but she never expounded. Frankly, I was terrified to ask. We laid there, conserving energy in each other's arms until a small ray of sunlight filtered through our window. I was able to see the cell now. It was small, only about six feet by six feet, with nothing but wood floors and a toilet behind a tattered curtain. The metal door was threaded with thick bars you'd be able to poke a finger through but nothing bigger. It gave me something to focus on as I dreamed of all the possible ways of escaping—not many.

Time passed, and the room got a little brighter, and the temperature slowly eased enough for us to sit up, claiming our own space sitting right next to each other. Our glances were shy at first, my cheeks heating when I thought about how we survived the night holding each other, but that's all it was—survival.

Because it wouldn't be anything else . . .

Wearing the same pants suit she'd been in since we crashed the boat, her hair was now a tangled mess on top of her head. Dark smudges of dirt lined her jaw, and cheek hollows had started to manifest, more than likely from days of not eating well. Despite her rumpled condition, there was a sparkle in her eye, outing a last little glimmer of hope.

Measured steps creaked all around us, and from the patterns and placements, I gathered there had to be at least a dozen pirates on this ship. As the light grew slightly brighter, familiar sounds came. Voices, and sounds like grinding metal.

And smells.

The undeniable scent of cooking food bubbled through the little window. Porridge of some sort, and smoked fish. My stomach rolled toward the smell, grappling for a connection to something—anything—of substance. As the aroma wafted stronger, and my stomach pangs turned to full belly aches, I fought the urge to cry out in tears, pleading for food. The agony was nearly unbearable, and I found myself rocking back and forth to soothe the bursts of pain. Just when I thought I would pass out again, a rattle sounded on our door, and the little window bars opened. Not all the way, but enough for a guard to push food through. He passed two small bowls, one by one, and Evie received them. After she set those on the ground next to me, he pushed two flasks through. As soon as the flasks were in her hands, the windows wailed shut, and the footsteps stomped away.

I no longer cared I was in jail. I was given a lifeline. Food to last another day, and best of all Evie was here with me, a loyal companion.

I stayed awake the whole day, studying the creeks of the boat, and patterns of footsteps. From what I could tell, it was normal sailing stuff. It didn't seem as if we were in immediate danger. We'd come so far, and I wasn't giving up hope now, even if I was in a pirate jail.

When evening came, my mind grew heavy, anxious for sleep, but the temperature quickly plummeted again, and the trembles came. I gazed at Evie with sleep-deprived eyes and held my arm for her. "You don't have to if you don't want to, and I more than likely smell worse than a garbage dump, but I'm happy to snuggle if you want to keep warm."

She immediately scooted over, laying her head on my chest, trapping in a pocket of warmth on that side of my body. It was enough to stop the quakes, but my breath didn't even out as it had done the night before. Instead, it went a notch farther, sending a whoosh of emotion to stir my heart. My brow lowered, as I concentrated on the tiny flutters that puttered against my chest right near Evie's head. Her sweetness crept over me, easing tension, creating a lighthearted feeling I'd never experienced. It made my brow soften, and the tips of my lips teased an upward bend. Despite our near-death situation, I *enjoyed* having Evie in my arms so much it warmed me even more, and I was actually able to relax on the wood floor, breathing easier than I'd ever remembered.

"I suppose it would be too much to ask the guard for a blanket," Evie's attempt at a joke made me smile.

"You tell me." My sleepy voice hummed, and even though we were literally rotting in a pirate jail cell, I was basking in Evie's touch. I've never felt something quite like this before. "What happened in the movie when they did that?"

"To be honest. I don't think they lived this long," Her voice was sullen, not as bubbly as her normal self, pricking at my conscious.

"Hey Evie." My throat had softened some over the day, and words were becoming easier, though they sounded hoarse. "How are you holding up?"

When she didn't reply, I lowered my gaze down to her face, a few inches from mine. I could only make out a few shadows of her face, but her breath was shallow against my chest, as if all her hope was being drained. "I don't know anymore."

Even in my weakened state I was pulled to comfort her, wrapping my arm around her shoulders tighter, only wanting to ease her fear. She'd been comforting me for days, and it felt cathartic to finally be able to be a safe space for her. "I have to think that they have a plan for us since they are feeding us."

"Slaves, probably," she whispered. "Just enough to keep us alive, but hungry enough we won't try to escape." Her voice was so serious, compared to her usual quirks and narration, and the listlessness tugged at my heart.

We'd been in survival mode for so long I had been unable to think about anything more than what was happening in the moment, but now, on reflection I recalled *this was all my fault*. All of this was over a stupid treasure map that I was never supposed to have. I had been so desperate for something of value to hold on to, that I'd risked both our lives. *Now who even knows what our fate is?*

And Evie, a victim in all of this hadn't once even yelled at me. If I were her, I'd scratch my eyes out. What I did to her wasn't fair at all, but she'd been the most loyal companion. Guilt engulfed my heart so thick it seeped into the threads of my soul. "Evie," I rasped out, immediately drawing her gaze to connect with mine. "I'm so sorry I got us into this mess, but if I ever get us out, I promise to make it up to you. I don't know how, but I'll find a way."

Neither one of us moved as we held onto each other as if our lives depended on it. Not sure if it was the cold, or a need for connection, but I was encouraged knowing that no matter what was in store for us, we were going through it together.

Sleep never came for me, the hunger pains fiercely clawed into my stomach walls, wrenching deep into my nerves. When a warm damp droplet fell on my shirt, I knew Evie was wide awake too. "Why are you crying?" It was a stupid question, that I already had the answer for, and I immediately scolded myself. "Never mind. I know why."

"I guess if I have to die," Evie paused before leaking another tear on my shirt, the stain of her sorrow seeped right into my chest, filling me with so much regret. If only I hadn't been only thinking of myself, and she'd never have been put in this situation. I never thought for a moment that death would be a consequence. "I'm fine with it, but I wish I had a chance to tell my family my side. I tore off in a fit of rage, trying to hold everything in to preserve what was left of my sister's wedding, but now I'm seeing things differently."

"How do you mean?"

"I don't think it's my job to always be the peacekeeper. Actually, I'd like to rephrase that. It's *not* my job to be the peacekeeper. As much as I like things to be drama free, and I love my family, I'm allowed to live my life, too. I'm also not perfect, as nobody is. They need to stop expecting so much from me. All I wanted was a normal life, but they were never happy with me unless I was showering them with gifts, which I could only afford if I was working."

"Interesting." My brows furrowed, as that's not at all how I'd ever imagined a real family to be. "I never had family, or anyone who cared what I did, but I always sort of romanticized it, envisioning people who had picture-perfect routines like getting donuts together on lazy Saturday mornings, and walking their Golden Retriever after dinner until the streetlights came on."

"I'm sorry to whine about it." She sniffed a few times, and at least for the time being no tears dropped on my shirt. "I must sound like a spoiled brat to you, but that's not at all what I had. I had family, but they only talked to me when they found out about auditions, they wanted me to go to, or needed some extra money to float them until payday. I would have loved a Golden Retriever to walk. I was never allowed any pet, because pets would have taken my *focus* off my career."

"I've heard Goldens are the best dogs, always accepting everyone." I closed my eyes, imagining the things I always did when I got lonely. Having a dog, who'd never leave my side, a loyal companion. Sure, I could have adopted one, but I never thought it was fair to make a sweet innocent dog live outside. Someday.

"You know, I still have your treasure map," Evie breathed out, her tone hinted of curiosity. "I thought they would take it from me when they captured us, but they said it was worthless. I had hoped to bargain for our lives with it, but it didn't work. What do you think they want from us?"

My mind wiped clean, all possible answers didn't make sense. "I really don't know."

The silence which dragged on echoed more loudly than anything I'd ever heard, giving both of us ample time to imagine all the possible outcomes. My mind was trained to avoid the bad, but I don't think that's the case for Evie. Another tear dropped onto my shirt, and a faint tremble rippled through her shoulders. "Don't cry," I whispered, feeling so much desire to comfort her, and I rubbed her back. "I wish I could go rewind all this, and I'd take it all back. I would have never put you in this danger."

"You didn't put me here. I had wanted to come."

"Yeah, after I conned you into hiring me to be your ship captain."

"That's not how it went at all." She hiccup-sniffed, before continuing, "I overheard those pirates talking about you. I heard all about their murder and looting, and I knew they weren't safe, but I also heard how you had gotten away with the treasure map. I so desperately wanted to find that treasure to prove to my family I was more than just an actress. As much as you were using me, I was also using you. This isn't your fault. We did this together."

I don't know why I laughed. It was uncanny, and so sad, but I sputtered out through my chuckle. "I guess we make one sorry example of a team, right?"

"Not right." Her chuckle was singular, more like a scoff. "We've survived this far. We can't be that bad. Plus, we've stayed together."

Together...the word slammed into my heart in a way I was unprepared to feel. It was the opposite of a gut punch, instead of deflating me, it pumped up my heart, making me feel as if I mattered to someone.

I mattered to Evie.

A smile of affection teased on the edges of my lips, and I was compelled to press a kiss to the top of her head. It was the perfect spot right on the crown, warm and cushioned with her silky hair. I guess it's the kind of kiss that happens when two people come together to comfort each other. My heart drummed hard against my rib cage as I waited for her reaction. She stilled for a moment before her shoulder rose again, and with sweet angelic infections, she said, "Thank you."

"You're welcome." I closed my eyes, feeling a little more at peace, and drifted into a light sleep.

# Thirteen

## Evie

The next morning, a miracle happened. The cell door flew open, and four large guards lined the way out, while the biggest one passed inside with ropes.

Okay, maybe I was exaggerating a little because I got carried away when the door opened. I was ahead of myself and hadn't yet seen the ropes. Let's back up. Not a miracle. We will call this the *plot twist.*

Knowing better than to fight them, I held my wrists behind my back, waiting to be tied. I assumed the guard would tie our legs, too. When he didn't, I gasped, recalling a movie I'd done. My veins frosted with ice. "They usually only leave your feet untied when they want you to walk the plank," I hissed to Jasper.

"Shush!" He elbowed me hard and gave me a warning look.

"Just saying," I whispered out of the strained corner of my mouth while I waited for the guard to tie his wrists. "It doesn't look good." I thought Jasper was going to insist I be quiet again, but instead he peered at me with pining eyes.

"Whatever is about to happen, Evie," he whispered, "we do it together."

"Ah." I wince, as I wasn't sure I wanted to do *everything* he did. If he walked the plank, and I found a way out, I might take it—

"Evie!" He fully got the hang of the deep rasp now, as the guard pushed him forward. "I'm not leaving you again. Not if I can help it." The guard shoved him around the corner, and all I heard was the word "together," and it echoed in my heart.

Two remaining guards tugged on my upper arms, while jabbing a machete against my back. I scrambled to stay on my feet as they moved briskly, but I hadn't walked for days, and my legs were Jell-O. The guards shuffled us down a narrow dark hall and up a creepy staircase until we made it to the deck, where my lungs screamed for deep inhalations of the fresh sea air. It was heaven, and I couldn't get enough of the breeze, but it was short lived as they continued to steer us to the front of the boat. Here, we climbed another small set of stairs into the wheelhouse. Just before they opened the door, the biggest guard holding Jasper said, "The captain will see you now."

*Why did that not sound as inviting as I had hoped?*

Terror sliced through my body, and I had an even harder time moving my feet, but my guards propelled me forward with more than a gentle nudge. We were pushed through the door, guards still intact and lined up in the back of the small wheelhouse, with the captain's chair still facing away from us.

His long gray hair—I doubted was ever washed with proper shampoo—snarled and weaved in all directions halfway down his bloated back. His hand steadily rested on the boat controls, with the missing pinky reminding me we weren't on a cruise.

My eyes rolled to the heavens. *This is awfully dramatic if you're going to push us overboard.*

Slowly, the captain removed his hand from the controls, and the chair swiveled until we saw a leathered face, narrow and with a knotted gray bread. He wrung his hands together in his lap but made no move to stand. "I'm Captain Gray Beard," he said with an even tone. "It seems you've run into a member of my crew back on the mainland, and you took our treasure map—"

"There wasn't any treasure," Jasper blurted out. "The box was empty, except for a mirror."

Captain Gray Beard bobbed his head slowly up and down. "I've sent every pirate on this crew after that treasure, and no one has ever been able to unlock the island."

Jasper's head jolted back, and he snuck a look at me. I swallowed hard, not sure what any of this meant.

"Tell me about yourself." Captain snarled his nose, his nostrils flaring out. "Where are you from?"

"Ah, n-nowhere really?" Jasper stuttered. "Or, um, actually, a lot of places."

Gray Beard tipped his ear closer as if for clarification. "Parents?"

"No, sir." Sweat beaded on Jasper's brow. I wished there was something I could do to help this conversation, but I knew better than to speak out of turn when there's a machete at my back.

"Everyone has parents." Maybe it was my imagination, but the captain's voice appeared to soften.

"Biological ones, yes." Jasper's voice was slow, yet respectful, but since I was used to his inflections, I could tell they were tinted with strong emotions. "I don't know them. I was in an orphan home since I was a baby—"

"How old are you?" Captain rushed.

"Ah, I don't know my exact birthday but I'm in my early twenties."

"I'm going to be honest with you." Gray Beard's tone was inquiring. "When you stole my map, I was prepared to kill you." His pause was so long, I had time for a double gulp.  "When we finally captured you, I was ready to make you walk the plank."

"Ahh!" I gasped, but quickly buttoned my lip. *I knew it!*

"My guard saw something on you—a brand."

Captain finally rose to his feet and sauntered across the wheelhouse. He didn't stop until he was standing behind Jasper, examining the scar below his ear. As he studied it, he grew more still, and his eyes sparked a tiny glisten. "It's a half of a figure eight."

Jasper's gaze fell to the floor, and he nervously shuffled his feet. Clueless to what Captain was talking about, I looked to Jasper, but he remained unbothered. "I have no idea where it came from."

"I do." Captain asserted in a calm voice, his feet not moving, while the glisten in his eyes grew. "It's from your mother."

"How would you know my mother?" Jasper's brows angled as if he wasn't buying that. "And why would my mother scar me?"

The captain's gaze wafted over Jasper, giving him another full once over. Tears brimmed his eyes when he continued, "Why don't I show you."

# Fourteen

# JASPER

Time stood still.

How could this be?

All my life, nobody had even mentioned my mom to me. I'd begged every foster parent I'd had. Desperate for a normal life, and a stable home, I scoured for any clue to who my real parents were.

And this filthy pirate played with my emotions. How dare he? It's one thing to capture me, but talking about my mom was cruel.

Narrowing my eyes, I stood motionless waiting for him to explain. Instead of talking, Captain Gray Beard turned his head and pulled his greasy hair back. It was hard to see anything other than the dirt-stained skin, but I was stubborn, fixing my eyes hard.

*And there it was.*

A scar, the mirror image of mine.

I never believed my scar was anything different than an accidental wound. If there ever was a thing as proof that it was intentional, this would be it.

"Are you telling me I'm a pirate," I half joked at the coincidence. Raising an eyebrow, I paused as I considered how resourceful and comfortable I was sleeping in a gondola.

"No, you are not a pirate." Our eyes met on the same horizontal plane. "But, you are my son."

"Woo." I took an involuntary step back, while Evie gasped. There's no way I heard that correctly. "What did you say?"

"It seems like another lifetime ago." He stuffed his hands in his trouser pockets and turned his gaze to the ground, almost remorsefully. "I held you once for the entire night after your mother gave birth."

"H-How?" I stuttered, not believing it. Yet, now that the words were out, there was a glint in his eyes that was familiar.

"Let's take a walk." He motioned to the guard with the machete in my back to walk out of the wheelhouse, and my other guard automatically moved to the captain's chair for a wheel watch. I cut a gaze at Evie, not wanting to leave her, but with knives jammed up both our backs, neither one of us had a hankering to protest.

I scurried to keep the tip of the knife out of my back, and the captain hung on my side. Together, we walked down the steps and paced around the deck in a circular pattern with me closest to the water's edge. I was quite sure my proximity to the edge was done as a precaution in case I tried to escape, but with no land in sight, and Evie in the wheelhouse, there was no way I'd take the risk of trying to flee.

"I met your mother when I was twenty-seven," Captain started, his voice was strong. "Back then I had a more respectable career as a cargo sailor, hauling imported goods from all over Italy to the Americas." His head turned toward the sea, taking on a faraway expression.

"Jaliyah was her name, and she was an Italian Goddess. I first laid eyes on her at the merchant square. She was laughing and singing with a whole group of kids. She wasn't a good singer, and her laugh wasn't anything special, but when I looked at her, a ping went right to my heart. I was instantly enamored by her. I walked up to the group of kids and told them I'd pay them each a silver coin if they could get her to go on a date with me. Those kids." Gray Beard threw his head back, chuckling. "They did not disappoint. One little boy even made up a poem. And she said yes. We went to dinner, and from that moment on, any time I was in that town for an overnight, we were inseparable. I didn't come around as often as I wanted because of my long voyages, and because of that, I never asked about her normal life. Part of me worried she was seeing other guys, and I wanted to believe she was all mine. I also felt like she deserved more than a guy who was only around once every three weeks. But we just got each other." He shrugged and quit talking like he was ending the story, but I was hooked.

"You can't stop there," I insisted. My heart was oddly still, unlike any time before. Usually, it was a bit bipolar, either ramping too high, or sinking too low. Maybe it was the shock of it all, but it was even. "Did you guys get married?"

"We did." He nodded, the gleam in his eyes growing. "My shipping route got changed, and it went from me being gone for twenty-one days, to one where I would be gone forty-five, and we both cried. I knew if I didn't ask her then I never would. She didn't even pause before she said yes. I bought a nice ring for my small wage, but that was when things started to get weird. I wanted to get married in the courthouse, but she insisted we have somewhere more private. That should have been my first clue, but I didn't care if we got married in the middle of a circus, I wanted to be with her. I said yes." He chuckled lightly, shaking his head. "She dragged a priest out to the forest in the middle of the night. We said our vows clandestinely under the stars, and the only witness she allowed was a woman she said was her childhood nanny—"

"You didn't think that was weird." I couldn't help but interrupt. There were so many warning signs. "Was she married already, or what was her deal?"

"She wasn't married, but she didn't want her family to meet me. I never understood it, but I also never asked. Whenever I tried to bring up her family, her eyes would grow cloudy. We were happy, so there wasn't a reason for me to push it. We were two newlyweds, and she came on the boat with me. And you know as they say, two became three, and she had an awful time delivering you. At one point, I didn't think she was going to make it. They called more doctors, and specialists. Somehow, we got a miracle, and you both lived. We were so tired, and it was the wee hours of the morning, and everything was blurred. I'm not sure what happened, and I'll never get the real answer. Maybe someone recognized her, or they read her hospital records, but in the middle of the night, her hospital room was stormed with soldiers, and they took her."

"What do you mean they took her?" My heart wasn't still anymore. It ramped up back into manic mode. "Where was I?"

"She had you in her arms and wouldn't let go. I was quickly banished and then branded as an outlaw, ordered to never return. I couldn't get a job in any country with this brand. I quickly became so bitter, taking to the seas to rob people. I told myself I'd be okay if your mother and you lived and had each other. The news spread fast about our child and her father wasn't happy. He ordered the same fate for you, and you were branded, and removed."

"W-What kind of barbaric practice was that?" I spit out with such disgust. "And who did her dad think he was?"

"He was the king." The captain turned to meet my eyes again. "I found out the day I read it in the paper that your mother was a princess, and you had royal blood."

I started to stutter out a rebuttal when a mirage I'd seen only in my dreams—but for some unsolved reason it never left—glittered in front of me. A woman's face with skin so smooth, I wouldn't believe she ever knew how to frown, looked down on me. She's dressed in the finest silk dress unlike anything I'd ever seen or felt, and part of the reason I knew she was only ever a dream.

I heart pounded out so many questions, but I was completely frozen.

Everything I had thought I had never known was now being unveiled. Now the real question: Does my mother care as much as I do?

# Fifteen

## Evie

The guards returned me to the cell, slamming the door so hard, the lock echoed when it clanged into place. Even though it was still day, and the same cell I'd been in the last week, it was much scarier without Jasper. Nobody gave me a clue as to what was going on, and the hours ticked by. My curiosity turned to concern, and then my concern morphed into panic.

What if they really did make him walk the plank?

I'd be here all alone, and I have no idea how to escape by myself.

When the heavy wood door opened down the hall, I held my breath until I saw Jasper's familiar face appear. I flattened my body against the wall, feeling the need to be guarded until the guards left again. Instead of returning to the cell, Jasper bobbed his head in and waved me forward. "Evie, come with me. They are letting us go."

No guards were with Jasper, and he dangled a giant key ring at his waste. Doing a double-take, I scanned both sides of the hall. I was never a scholar, but one thing I'd learned was that pirates couldn't be trusted. It seemed too good to be true. My eyes raked his body, looking for a clue of deception, but

Jasper wasn't even tied up anymore. I hung back in the cell, not trusting the situation yet. "What's going on?"

"I talked to Captain Gray Beard, and he's letting us go. We're docking here shortly."

"Docking where?" I scrambled forward, as disbelief circled my brain, and my body moved instinctively toward him, not stopping until I grabbed his hand. It's how we'd spent the last week, hand in hand. When his eyes hit mine, there was a warmth that hadn't been there before, and he smiled at me, a rare genuine smile that said, "everything is going to be fine."

"What happened on your walk?" I gushed out, everything about Jasper's demeanor had seemed to change as if the dull gray cloud that had been following him around since I'd met him had been lifted.

"Something important came up. I hate to be so vague, but I need to take care of some business tonight—alone."

Alarms sounded in my head but cascaded to my heart. He said *I*. Before we left this cell this morning, he insisted we were doing everything together. Now after he'd made friends with a pirate, he's back to saying I. Was he planning to ditch me after I'd stayed by him through everything?

"Just you are going?" My gaze was a bit scrutinizing, but I tried not to act the part of the jealous girlfriend. I had no desire to hang out on a pirate ship all by myself.

"I told you; I'm not leaving you anymore." Still holding my hand, he reached his other hand out, taking both my hands together, pulling them close to his chest. The gesture was smooth, and unlike him in every way, while twisting my intestines into a southern backroad of curves. "I said everything we do is together. I intend to keep that promise, but unfortunately this is risky business, and I can't put you in harm's way again."

"Where are you going?" My heart was sinking fast as the promise he had just made me was already a memory.

"We're going to a dock at a small island off the coast of Italy, not that far from home. I'd like you to return home, where you are safe and comfortable. I'll come find you when I know it's safe."

There was no amount of chin tapping that could help me solve this sudden change of events. These pirates were chasing us for days with every intention of killing us, and now we're getting released. "Are you sure we can trust these people?"

"Evie." His voice grew raspy, as one hand dropped to my waist. "I can't promise that this isn't a setup, but I need to trust that you are safe at home while I see this through."

He had my heart on a yo-yo string, lifting it up, and then jerk dropping it back down. So much had happened since I left home, that I wasn't sure if it would feel like home anymore. Jasper had started to feel like home, but now he was back to acting shadowy again. Maybe I couldn't trust him?

"I think," I started slowly, still unsure of what I thought, but I didn't like the way my heart was being jerked around. "I'm ready to go home," I breathed out, instantly feeling a release. "If you have business to take care of, then do that. After you're done, come find me." Maybe it was a challenge? Would he care to look me up after we'd gone our separate ways?

Was our bond only a trauma bond we'd both soon forget?

We were about to find out.

After we docked, Jasper was quiet when he walked me through the wharf and hailed a cab. You'd think I'd be relieved to be on dry land, but there was so much uncertainty in the air, I wasn't sure if this was a goodbye, or it really was *goodbye*.

All of my I.D.'s and money had sunk with my boat, but I was able to use the cab driver's phone to log into my digital bank and prepay for my ride. Once the exchange was done, he was ready to go.

But I wasn't.

"How will I find you?" I asked, still holding Jasper's hand the way I'd been doing for days now.

"I'll find you." His eyes roamed my face, the inflections had transformed so much over the last hour. Between the sea beside him, and the skies above us, the spirals of blue were achingly gorgeous. But it was deeper than that. It was a connection, like a secret club that we both belonged to. I wasn't ready to say goodbye. My chin quivered, the stress of the last few days rose into my throat. The fear, the hunger, the pain, the exhaustion, and something I'd never anticipated feeling, the heartbreak.

This was silly.

He was never mine.

I was hushed, feeling all my feelings, when he tipped my chin up with his finger, and whispered, "Evie, don't be scared. I'll find you." His gaze bounced from my eyes to my lips, and without hesitation I took the hint, and leaned forward. The inflections in his eyes softened even more as he lowered his chin to meet me halfway.

My eyelids lowered when our lips folded together in a cautious, first kiss, hinting at a possibility of something more. His lips were soft, asking permission, tugging at mine in the most tender way. I couldn't help but wonder if everything we went through was fate's way of bringing us together. Our bond was the first seedlings of something greater, and my heart wrenched when I thought about the possibility of Jasper leaving, and never finding me. The moment was perfection.

The cab honked, jolting us apart, and my heart sank lower as I forced my lip inward and smiled shyly. "Don't worry. I'll find you." Jasper echoed as I turned toward the cab, and got in. He shut the door as soon as my feet were tucked safely inside. Ha! I scoffed at the thought of my feet being safe again. It was everything I wanted, so why did I feel broken?

# Sixteen

## Jasper

I watched the cab shrink over the horizon, feeling *even*. I attributed the feeling of evenness as peace, which was brand new to me. It didn't come from leaving Evie, as that put my heart in a chokehold. If anything, it came from having Evie, a person to connect with. I hated leaving her with all this uncertainty, but she couldn't come where I was going. I didn't want to apprise her of the details, and that's why I was ambiguous. Plus, she went home to a warm bed, food, and all the amenities, which was the best thing for her.

*I can't wait to join her.*

Now I have a new mission.

To find my mother.

I sort of had a plan, but it had a few potential flaws. First, I was going to hitch a ride—or walk if I couldn't find a random stranger to pick me up—to the palace, at which point I would stroll right up to the golden gate and knock.

My gaze slid to the side, as I already knew that wouldn't work. They would never let a homeless thief on their grounds, let alone give me a chance to talk to the queen.

How about a disguise?

I could find a mailman shirt or something. I pondered as I sauntered past the businesses on the wharf and headed toward the palace. I'd never been to this little country before, but it wasn't hard to navigate as the palace loomed high over the village on a hill, standing taller than any other structure. It really was an impressive architectural masterpiece, with its ivory towers and spirals of windows that seemed to wrap to the sky.

I cut through an alley and came out in a clearing filled with vendors, resembling something like a street carnival. Food trucks and drink carts lined the road, and everything from face painting booths to jugglers took the main stage in the center. My stomach churned, begging for a taste of the decadent smell. The old me would have snuck behind a hotdog cart and helped myself, but something in me had changed. It didn't give me the same thrill. I pushed my rumbles aside and continued.

Cheerful music piped out, and kids and elderly alike all danced in a circle. They clapped, they stomped, they bowed to their neighbor, and took their hands and twirled. I stood back watching, thinking about what a happy little village this seemed to be. I had the steps about memorized when it dawned on me. This was the merchant square Captain told me about. This was exactly what he had seen when he'd wandered off his boat all those years ago. It must just be a Saturday tradition to gather in the square, that never fell away, even after all these years.

With candy-colored houses, and cobble stone streets, it was the quaintest village I'd ever seen, and it was certainly enjoyable to stroll through. My gaze swept both ways as I crossed the street, turning on the white pebble path leading to the palace road. My palms started to sweat, as I only had so much time to figure out something persuasive to say to get me inside. Yet, I knew I could do it. After escaping death so many times this last week, I wasn't intimidated by this.

Okay, maybe I was getting cocky?

A mere peptalk.

In the past, my arrogance had been my demise.

Today, I squared my shoulders back, put one foot in front of the other, and set my sight on the palace...An ordinary laugh that was nothing special wafted from the center of the dancing circle, halting my steps.

*Nah, it can't be.*

I slid my foot out, ready to continue but the laughter bubbled again. This time it sent a spear right through my heart, and I pivoted quickly without it ever registering in my brain that I started jogging back down the hill. My ears were so attuned to it, as if an invisible string was reeling me in, and I didn't stop until I was standing in the back of the sea of dancers, still unable to get eyes on *her*.

What does she look like?

Will she even remember me?

I had no clue what I'd say, but I was standing on my toes, stretching my neck tall, yearning for a glimpse as I wove through the tightly packed crowd. My breath rushed in fast and heaved out faster as everything was unfolding like a fairytale. I finally made it to the front row and steeled my gaze forward, prepared to hold my breath, but it came easy. Looking at her was easier than anything I'd done in my life.

She was certainly regal, her beauty still evident despite the years, and survival of a heartbreak that would kill many. With perfect posture, she was tall, almost as tall as me. Her eyes shimmered sea green and were framed by wispy strands of silver hair which had fallen from her full crown-wrapped bun. Her eyes caught mine, and for a moment I thought they would stay frozen together, but she quickly passed over me. She turned to the child by her side, asking about the child's schooling. I closed my eyes, and let her voice wrap about me, and I was sinking into a pile of feather pillows, already warmed.

"Your Majesty." I hadn't planned on speaking out, but that invisible string was pulling so tight, and I couldn't risk it breaking another time.

Her eyes swept back to me. "How do you do?"

My lips were putty, so dry and hard to mold into words. I ran my tongue over them, hydrating them. "My father has sent something for you." I pulled the wrinkled map out of my satchel, still amazed it even looked like a map after everything it had been through. With trembling fingers, I held it out for her to see.

Her gaze dropped, and so did her expression. All color drained from her face before her eyes sprang wide back to me, panic etched in all the features of her face. "Where did you get this?"

"My father," I repeated. "You sent it to him."

"I don't believe it." Her hand slipped over the map as she whisked it away from me, and gently pressed it to her heart. Her eyes glistened back. "Your father?"

I nodded as tears jabbed at the back of my eyes, but I held onto them and quietly bowed my head. The crowd hushed, everyone fanning around, watching us. It was as if she was reminded we weren't alone because she passed her gaze to the side, and then curtly smiled at me. "What is your name, sir?"

"Jasper Night."

"Night is an interesting surname. Where abouts is your father from?"

"It's not my father's surname. I was told I was given the name because I showed up in the orphanage in the middle of the night, in a bundle, with a note that said, my name was only Jasper. The aids started calling me Jasper of the Night, and eventually it became Jasper Night."

Her free hand lifted to shield her other hand still holding her heart and her bottom lip rolled under her top where she pitched it tightly, before forcing a tight smile. Again, her eyes flew to the crowd around us, and she whispered, "Can we talk somewhere else?"

"Of course." Fear ripped through my body. Now, afraid she was embarrassed by me, standing here in my rags, I started to wish I had cleaned up first. However, I didn't have anything to clean up into. She more than likely wanted to tell me to leave her alone while also not wanting to make a scene. "This is not my village. I have nowhere to offer, as I'm only passing through, but we can walk?"

"Thank you all for sharing your afternoon with me." She stuck her hand out to wave to her friends, politely calling out, "It's getting late, and I'm going to visit with my guest."

Most of the crowd had already lost interest in her since she had stopped paying attention, and the guards that had been standing behind her automatically moved to follow us. Her eyes caught them both, and without having to request a change of pace, they instinctively understood to hang back more than a few steps, and we all moved together down the cobblestone street toward the palace.

Her steps were light and graceful, and the farther we moved away from the crowd, her expression shifted to one of warmer inflections. "My heart is pounding too fast," she started once we were out of hearing range. "I'm going to cut to the chase. I know who you are. You look just like my father." She tried to stifle her cries by pressing her petite palm over her mouth, but it didn't conceal her quivering jaw. "How are you?"

Stunned, I didn't have words. I had assumed she'd be full of questions, wondering how I found her or what I wanted from her. I hadn't thought for a moment the first one would be her asking about *me*. So many nights I'd laid awake, dreaming of this moment. I always assumed my mother never cared how I was.

I didn't dare tell her who I really turned out to be— a thief.

Even though I'd just met her, I wasn't ready to see shame in her eyes.

She would turn me away, and I craved another moment with her, enough to imprint a seed of something I could carry with me. "I'm well." It came out sounding more like a question, and the widening of her eyes told me she didn't really believe it.

"And your childhood?" Her voice was tiny. "Was it happy?"

An itch sprang up behind my ear, and I scratched it, taking the time to reply. I'd never been a liar, and I just couldn't go down that road again after everything with Evie.

"Oh my." Her eyes locked on my scar. "That's what they did to you when you were just a baby." She blinked in rapid succession, but it no longer held back the tears, as each blink pulled down a single tear. "I never had a choice to give you away. I searched for years, and it was like they'd hidden you from me. There hasn't been a day that I haven't thought about you." She shook her head back and forth, letting the tears cascade freely now. Maybe I expected my mother to be more closed off, and private, but she wasn't that way at all. She honestly just looked broken.

Like me.

Only in nicer clothing.

She opened her arms slightly, as if not to get her hopes up too much. "Can I hug you?"

It was like the hands of time rewound, giving grace to all the moments we never shared, and I stepped forward to embrace her.

She never asked me what I wanted from her.

Call it a mother's intuition, but I felt she just knew I didn't want any-*thing* but to know her, and her willingness to let me in was evident from that first embrace.

"You have to come back to the palace with me." My mother beckoned me forward as she strolled down the pebbled path. "I have so many things to show you."

Blinking, I did my best to wake from this dream, because I couldn't imagine the disappointment I'd feel if this continued to unfold perfectly, and I'd wake up later.

Nothing changed.

I stood on solid ground staring at my mother beaming back at me, and I breathed a little lighter as I stepped in unison with her. I was going to the palace with my mother, two things I never in my life thought I would say.

The palace was a palace, was a palace. There's not much more you can say but that. It was exactly how you'd picture a place where royalty lived. From its high cathedral ceilings with gold and crystal chandeliers hanging in *every* room, to the huge grand halls, and spiral staircases. I fought to keep my jaw from hanging open. Everything about it was grand, and my mother passed through the halls with her chin up as if she hardly noticed her surroundings were anything unusual.

Servants bustled around cleaning, and a personal maid seemed to come out of nowhere as soon as we passed through the front entrance. She was waiting ready to replace Mother's outdoor shoes with warm slippers. The place ran like a well-oiled machine, and my eyes panned over each room we passed, awe filling my chest.

Did I feel like I missed out on something?

Maybe a little.

Okay, that's a huge understatement.

Confusion throbbed in the front of my brain. How in the world did I grow up so completely opposite to my mother? My heart sank as we passed through yet another chamber. This one filled with walls of museum-worthy canvas paintings and marble sculptures. I had always assumed my mother had been too poor to raise me.

This was quite the opposite.

Not humbling at all.

In fact, it was infuriating.

Surely, there'd would have been some tiny corner in this place that I could have lived as I didn't require much. She had every resource in the entire country at her fingertips, and nobody could say boo about it because she was the queen. Chewing the inside of my cheek, I stayed silent as death when we passed into yet another room, this one smaller than the last with a rich crimson rug in the center of the room, and a Queen Anne desk in front of the large bay window. Here, she slowed her steps, shutting the solid wood door behind her, and turned to gaze to me. "This is my private office. All my staff know they aren't to interrupt. It's the only place I can really speak openly. Come," she waved me farther into the room, motioned for me to sit on one of the high-back chairs, "make yourself comfortable. We have so much to talk about."

"Where do we start." I promptly sat exactly where she had pointed, not wanting to do anything to wear out my welcome before I was ready to leave.

The chair cushion was so soft, I sunk right down into it, feeling a heaviness encapsulate my whole body.

She gracefully sat in the chair opposite me, taking the time to tuck her dress perfectly beneath her but she didn't raise her gaze when she started, "I'd like to start with an apology."

I waved dismissively. "No, there's no need—"

"Please." Her face stilled, waiting for me to allow her the space to talk, and I buttoned my lip before she went on, "I wasn't in this position when I had you, as I was under my father's rule." Her gaze took a faraway expression. "This would have been so different if only the timing was better."

"It's *fine*, really," I squeaked out. So many nights I slept under the stars as that was my only option, and I dreamed of all the fake identities I could give myself to give a face to my real family. Never in a million years could anybody convince me my mom was an actual queen. Yet, the most surprising thing is that I had empathy for her situation.

"It's not fine, but it is what it is." Her eyelids appeared heavy as she raised her gaze to meet mine again. "My father passed away a year ago. With me being the only heir, taking the crown was an easy transition for me. I never married again, as I never had my first marriage dissolved. I willingly took the throne as governing gives me a way to give back, and nobody is making decisions for me anymore."

Swallowing, my brow furrowed as I tried to hear the words she wasn't speaking. "I can't make up for lost time," she went on, "life is short, and I hate to waste any more of the precious time we've been given. What would you say about moving into the palace with me, and getting to know the life that was stolen from you?"

My brows shot to the ceiling, and I leaned forehead as her invitation rung around my head. That can't be right. "Pardon me?" I sputtered out.

"No pressure of course, and if you don't find it comfortable, you may leave whenever." A light blush crept down her cheek. "I realize you aren't a child anymore, and you certainly have your own life, but I want to offer you the chance to try to regain what is rightfully yours."

Am I dehydrated?

Is this what happens when you accidentally swallow too much salt water, because I actually love this sensation.

Give me all the salt water.

"Did you hear me?" My mother leaned forward, tilted her head a measure closer.

"Yeah, I heard you but I'm a little stunned."

"It's a lot to consider, and again, I would never ask you to abandon your life but maybe for a while—a vacation perhaps—and we can get to know each other."

Of course, I didn't have a life to abandon. There's nobody ever waiting on me, well except for this one time there is actually...*Evie.*

My stomach knotted as I recalled our insane week together, leaving us both in a place where we didn't really know what we were to each other. I wanted more than anything to continue on the path of connection with Evie, but she's a famous actress. Would she even really care to hang out again once she gets back into her amazing life?

"We must have a celebration," she cut in, a smile growing on her lips. "A ball to announce to the country that you are alive, and inline for the throne. Everyone will be invited, and no expense will be spared." She placed a palm over her chest before leaning forward, "Sorry, I keep getting ahead of myself. I should have asked if you have a wife, or a family. Anyone who is a family of yours, is welcome as well."

"I'm not married," I started slowly, not having any idea how to explain Evie as we hardly knew each other. "But there is this one person, Evie is her name, and she's...*special*?" My voice ticked up at the end, as if I was asking a question, and one I wanted an answer, too. I wanted to know what Evie was to me.

"Wonderful." My mother clapped her hands together in front of her, sealing the conversation. " We can send for her. I can't wait to meet her."

My gaze dropped, now unable to visualize how that conversation would even work. How would I explain all this to Evie? Would she think I lied to her, or was currently lying, because there is no way, I would believe this. "I, ah, would love that," I added firmly, my heart swelling so full at all the thoughts of Evie *possibly* coming here.

In all the dreams I dared to dream over the years, nothing was as amazing as all of this had the potential to be. If only it goes the way that I hoped...

# Seventeen

## Evie

One benefit about looking like you're the last contestant left on the season of Survivor was that no one recognized me. I had an effortless time riding that cab to my private villa. All my security gates and doors were controlled by a code, and I easily let myself in. Within moments, I was absorbed back into my old life. Except for thousands of missed emails, and messages, but I left it all to sit another day.

The main thing I wanted was a long warm shower with all the cleanest-smelling soaps I could find all lathered together. I took my time, relishing every ounce of water and letting go of the stress, as the layers of dirt rinsed off me.

Then I put on my most basic white cotton pajamas, and I glanced in the mirror. Even with the double application of conditioner, my hair was still tangled, and I searched in my drawer for a pick, and set about gently combing the knots out. It was a robotic task that gave my mind room to wonder, and I couldn't shake off the feeling of unease about leaving Jasper. I hoped he'd hadn't headed back to the streets. What if his "risky business" he didn't want to include me in was more thievery? Did he know another way to get money? I was more than willing to help him find suitable work and living arrangements, even if he didn't want to be with me. He's too good of guy to live that life.

After I got the tangles out of my hair, I headed to the kitchen. Despite the early evening light streaming through the large arched window of my front room, a sense of foreboding hovered over my thoughts. I just couldn't shake it. I took a deep breath and moved to the pantry. Ravenous, I grabbed a jar of peanut butter from the pantry, and big spoon from the silverware drawer and took half spoonful bites at a time.

I hummed as I swallowed; nothing had ever tasted so good in my life.

When my stomach finally calmed, I made my way over the window.

The sun crested over the tall city buildings, sending out golden fingers to touch the world below. In a way it felt like it was teasing me, reminding me of all the world out there I had just left. I had always been content to bask in this city view before, but tonight something was off.

I should feel safe, locked inside my home in my private gated community.

Anxiety pumped through my veins, and a tremor of unease sliced through my gut, spreading a sense that something was not right.

Yet, Jasper wasn't an ordinary guy. I couldn't call him to talk, and he didn't have an address. Part of me wished I'd insisted he'd come back with me, but the conviction was strong in his eyes that he had some business to take care of.

I hoped when he was done with whatever it was, he would return to find me.

I turned away from the window, letting my own reality sink in. I had my own business to take care of too, starting with my sister. Out of all the messages that I'd gotten while I was gone, not one of them was from her. I understood I wasn't gone that long, and she'd likely just be returning from her honeymoon. She didn't have a clue what I'd been through this last week, but in her defense it's not like they would have had a way to find out.

The crazy thing was that I never even wanted to be in any spotlight. I did that because my parents pushed me into it when I was a child. I'd give it all up if I had any other clue what I wanted to do with my life. This week away showed me a lot about the strength I had that I never gave myself credit for, and I was committed to living my life my way.

So the yacht didn't work out...

Sighing, I pushed all my random worries away. Finally, after so many nights away, I went to order a large amount of Chinese take-out, and rest in my own bed until it was delivered.

I'd like to say I heard from Jasper the very next morning, and we quickly became inseparable, but that didn't happen. The morning came, and no word from him.

The next day came, and still nothing.

Long days turned into a week, and I needed to make some decisions about my life.

First, I filed an insurance claim on my yacht. That felt rather nice.

Next on the list was to pay a visit to my sister. Or maybe I'd just call? I paced my living room, as I really didn't want to do either.

I could email.

The thing with email, though, is that you don't know if they received it, and she could certainly deny she read it.

If she was going to reject me again, I would need to hear with my own ears to have closure. I dropped a heavy sigh, as my heart needed to see her in person. Once my mind was made up, I gathered my things and left. The drive over was nerve wracking. Every little bubble in the road seemed to poke at my nerves, intensifying the stress already coursing through my body.

Seeing her car parked outside her home, I tensed even more as I pulled in behind it, and got out. I tried to act casually as I meandered up her narrow driveway, my heart pounding out warning beats, saying don't get your hopes up. Elizabeth had been awfully serious when she said she never wanted to see me again, and the hateful expression on her face flashed through my mind, giving me pause at her front door. I took a deep breath and knocked.

My eyes scanned the yard nervously. I couldn't help but wonder what her reaction would be. Would she be angry? Indifferent? Or perhaps... relieved? The door opened, and Elizabeth was there, staring at me with her arms across her chest.

I gave a hopeful smile as I watched my younger sibling glare at me through clenched teeth. We used to be so close in our younger years, but as my fame grew, so did the distance between us. I wanted us back so much. I couldn't help but feel a twinge of envy at how simple Elzabeth's life was, compared to the responsibilities that weighed heavily on my shoulders. "I know you don't want to see me." I held up my hand, pleading for her to give me some time. I looked into her eyes that matched mine in color and shape, trying to convey the depth of my regret, not for what I did, because I didn't really do anything wrong. I was just deeply sad how everything turned out. "I'm sorry," I whispered, my voice cracking with emotion.

Her expression softened slightly, but a flicker of hurt remained in her gaze. I dropped my hand to her arm, hoping for forgiveness. "I never meant to steal your thunder. Please, let me make it right." With bated breath, I waited for her response, knowing that the fate of our relationship hung delicately in the balance.

Elizabeth's shoulders rose in inhalation. "I appreciate the apology, but it'll take time for me to truly get past it."

I nodded, understanding that I couldn't change anything. "I know. I'll do whatever it takes to make things better," I repeated earnestly.

Part of me was hopeful that she'd immediately invite me in for coffee, and we'd chat like best friends, but that didn't happen. I knew that rebuilding our relationship would be an arduous journey, but I fully believed it was worth fighting for. And that was that.

As I drove back home, I was reminded of so many of the little moments we shared as children, and I wasn't ready to let those go. I would fight every day to support my sister. I wasn't happy about how it turned out, but I wasn't as sad about it anymore. I was even.

I pulled into my driveway, the surprising sight of some sort of military guard sitting on my doorstep. My already heightened anxiety soared as I pondered all the terrible reasons this man would be here. I don't have anything to do with the army. "Good morning, sir," I call as I shut my car door, and strode forward. "What can I do for you?"

Standing lean, with his heels clicked together he spoke with a projection in his tone. "I have an invitation for you from the Queen of Nuvolla to attend a royal ball."

"Never heard of that place." My gaze skirted to the side, as I get a lot of random invites to things, being a celebrity and all. The political ones are the hardest to turn down. I hate to make an enemy of an entire nation, but I had no clue where this place was.

"It's a small island, and it's a wonderful place. Nuvola actually means "cloud" in Italian and truly feels like a little cloud of paradise."

"It sounds lovely." I pursed my lips, as I contemplated how to politely decline. "Er, I'm taking a bit of a sabbatical, I've had a lot going on, and you can tell your queen I'm completely flattered, but I can't fit it in."

"Very well," he huffed, stiffening his shoulders even more. "I'll report back, but I assure you she will not be happy to hear this."

"I'm sorry." I blinked, wondering why this felt so personal. I have no idea who this person is, and I can't randomly accept invitations. "I'll take the invitation and consider it, but I'm almost certain I can't fit it in." I reached out to receive his white sealed envelope. He spun on his heels and started to saunter down my driveway when my breath hitched in my chest.

The envelope had a wax seal with half of a figure eight, and a heart—exactly like one I'd seen before. "Wait," I ran after him, "where did you get this?"

"The Queen of Nuvola has sent it to you." His expression was flat.

"You said that," I rushed out, my heart beating hard against my ribcage, "But what is this seal?"

"It's the royal seal." He seemed bored with my question, but humored me, "the dynasty has used it for over a hundred years."

Goosebumps jutted up my spine as I stared ominously at the envelope. I had no idea who the Queen of Nuvola was, but I didn't doubt this had everything to do with the quest I had just completed. Do I dare do this alone? I scanned up and down the street, wishing this was a fairytale, and Jasper would come riding up on a white horse to assist me.

He wasn't here.

I was alone with a decision to make all by myself.

One that could change my life forever.

What if it's more pirates?

I winced, pushing that thought out of my head, and a small smirk grew on my lips.

*There's only one way to find out.*

# Eighteen

## Evie

Checking the invitation seal again, I ran my finger over the raised crimson wax and swallowed. This could go so many ways. So many possible *bad* ways, but with no word from Jasper, this is the closest thing I had to a clue.

I was taking it.

Life doesn't happen when you're shut up in a luxury condo.

I slipped on my heels, one at a time, taking care to buckle the strap at my ankle. When I stood, I made sure my dress hemline hit the floor perfectly. I'd never been to a royal ball. Although I pretended many times for TV. I did what I always do when I'm a fish out of water—act.

I stuck one toe in front of the other, pretending to balance a book on my head with perfect posture and slipped out the front door. With no pumpkin carriage waiting for me, I slid into the driver's seat of my Mercedes and settled in for the three-hour drive south. With a forty-two-ounce water jug, and an audiobook downloaded on my phone, I was ready to go.

I had the top down on my car, not because it was nice out. It was cloudy, and a tad windy, but hey, you only live once, and I was so ready to live this life I'd been scared to live. If that meant I had to feel the elements on a day that wasn't perfect, I lifted my chin and breathed into it. I giggled as the cloud directly overhead grayed even more, threatening rain. After the month I'd had, rain wouldn't shadow me. It would make a memory of the best kind.

I thought my heart was racing on my way to visit Elizabeth, but that was nothing. Now it pounded like a bass drum. I had no confirmation that this had anything to do with Jasper, but every ounce of my soul told me to trust my gut and drive. My GPS took me south, and over a narrow bridge I never knew existed, to a twisty road that seemed to wind into the clouds. When I wound around the other side, I pulled into a clearing of a small, quaint little village, overlooked by the most beautiful castle sitting on the highest butte.

Since that's where my GPS was taking me, that's where I drove. The golden gate was wide open, and I drove through it to be immediately stopped by guards. They looked more like Nutcracker dancers than any sort of military defender, with tall hats and redcoats. The tallest guard leaned over my door, and politely asked with the cutest accent, "May I see you invitation please?"

I passed over my envelope, and he took one look at it before stuffing it into his front pocket, and stepped back from my car, granting permission, "You may pass."

I pulled forward, following the winding road to a parking lot, where dozens of cars had already filled the first two rows. I pulled into a spot without any trouble and stepped out of my car.

Music wafted from the courtyard. Music with whimsical string instruments that seemed to know every note that love was made of made my heart pound in my chest, and strong brass horns bringing in the alto tones made the blood in my veins pump with excitement. The tiniest flute tooted out a little melody that made me visualize a butterfly fluttering around, and the whole musical ensemble made this little courtyard come alive.

Couples strutted together with matching outfits of the finest fabric, while clearing the center aisle that led to the castle. I rounded the corner, setting my gaze on the castle, and everything seemed to play out like a movie, with the shimmering gleam of the castle setting in the background.

And there he was...

Standing in long coattails, and a fresh new haircut, nothing about him was unrecognizable because I'd know that face anywhere. Our eyes met first, drawn to each other like magnets. His eyes were a mixture of joy and uncertainty. He hesitated for a moment before stepping toward me, and I picked up my pace as I walked toward him. Time seemed to standstill as we took each other in, both searching for answers in the depths of each other's gaze.

Next came the confusion.

Everything about this scene was not what I had envisioned, and nothing at all like what Jasper had said his life was like. He'd never even mentioned Nuvola before. With a deep breath, he finally spoke, breaking the silence that hung heavily between us. "Evie."

A rush of anxiety pumped through my veins as I continued my way towards him, knowing that this was the moment I had been waiting for—the minute when everything would change. "I'm so confused right now."

The way we stood close together, our bodies practically touching, created an undeniable chemistry that spoke loudly about what we both had on our minds.

"Evie, I brought you to this village for a reason." He cleared his throat, and I watched the wonder dance across his features before he continued, "I know this is going to be shocking, but I swear it's the truth. You know how I grew up as an orphan."

"That's what you said." I chewed the bottom of my lips as everything about his demeanor told me he was about to confess a lie.

"I recently reconnected with my birth mother. Her father had forced her to give me up for adoption, but now he's passed away. The shocking part is that my mom is the queen of this country, which means...I'm a prince."

My eyes widened, as this had to be the most absurd thing I'd heard this month, and I'd heard an awful lot of crazy things this month. "A prince?" A little giggle of disbelief bleeped out from her lips. "Like, from a real royal family?"

He nodded, his gaze holding firm on me. "Yes, I'm sorry I kept this from you, but I waited to tell you until I knew what it actually meant for us." He reached for my hand, swooping it up until it was next to his heart. "This is for real. I'm the only heir."

"Okay. That's certainly an interesting plot twist that didn't happen in the movie." My skeptical smile spread across my face. Before I could laugh, my lashes lowered. "Well, I don't care about your title."

His eyes filled with love, longing, and so many spirals that gave me all the feels. In that moment, I knew that I had found my true partner. One who'd love me unconditionally, prince or not.

"I meant what I said when I said I never wanted to leave you." He placed one hand on my hip, sending a spark right to my heart.

*We had the same idea.*

Neither of us hesitated, as we were living out our own fairy tale and our lips met in an embrace, the world fading away as the music played in the background, the melody of the flute fluttering lightly. Kissing him was like finding my perfect counterpart, the one who knew me *for me*. The sun could have fallen from the sky, and I wouldn't have noticed, as our lips melted together, one languid caress at a time.

When we pulled away, we smiled shyly as we knew our friendship had been transformed into something deeper. We were standing on the threshold to a new chapter in our lives, one filled with adventure, uncertainty, and the possibility of love, but definitely no pirates.

And with that, I knew I was finally done acting. No more pretending. My love for Jasper was real, and I was ready to live.

We were living our best lives.

# Epilogue

## Jasper

I rolled the tattered parchment paper and stuffed it into an empty wine bottle. After replacing the cork, I handed it to Evie. "You do the honors."

"Are you sure you want to do this?" Her eyes, more beautiful than the sea before us, held a warning. "I'd actually prefer you to do it."

"Yeah, that map has a purpose. It's clearly bringing soulmates together, and it's time we pay it forward." I wound my arm all the way back and flung the bottle as hard as I could. We watched it sail through the sky, arching high before it plopped down into the sea current heading the opposite direction.

"I thought you said your mother gave the map to your father." Evie's brows beaded together.

Reaching out to take her hand in mine, my heart skipped a beat as our fingers glided together. "She did. She said after her dad found it on one of his voyages across the Holy Land, that at first, he assumed it was a farce, but it clearly worked for him, and others. He stored it in a chest in the palace, not wanting anyone to find out about his find. Being mischievous my mother had found it in her youth, and when they took me away, she stole the map, praying that it would work to bring me back."

The sun was setting behind us, disappearing behind the rolling hills we'd come to love in this village. The air between us was steeped with anticipation as we held each other's gazes.

I was used to being alone my whole life. Never did I dream I'd meet both my parents, and the love of my life in the same year, or even at all. But deep down, I longed for something even deeper, a connection that made Evie and me real family.

This was it.

Evie was everything, and I knew it with everything in me.

Now that the map was off to find a new destiny, there was only one thing left to do to finish this story. I got down on one knee and pulled a velvet box out of my jacket. It was an heirloom from my mother's collection, and worth more money than most countries, but the money didn't matter to me. The only thing I cared about was making Evie see that this togetherness thing was real, forever and eternal.

Evie's eyes rounded with tears welling up as the sparkling diamond ring glistening in the sunlight. I had rehearsed this moment so many times in my head, but the words caught in my throat, and my voice cracked. "Evie, I meant it when I said I want to do everything together. Will you marry me?"

Evie gasped in delight. Without hesitation, she whispered, "Yes."

I slid the ring on her finger, and leaned in for a kiss, our lips bonding, and breaths mingling as we had learned to breathe each other in, being one. I was freefalling, and life could never get better than this. Our embrace filled with longing, my fingers tangled in her hair as we held onto each other tightly. When I pulled away, my smile was growing. My days of thievery were over. Not because I had found my riches, but I had been given a deeper purpose. All I wanted to do was live each day to make Evie proud of me.

One could say my luckiest loot had been that map, but I knew better than that. Of all the things I'd stolen, the most valuable prize was the key to Evie's heart.

That was the real treasure, and I was going to guard it with my life.

"Now that this is settled." I twisted the ring on her finger and playfully winked at her as a warning, "Let's talk about getting a Golden Retriever."

She threw back her head in laugher, as we both knew I won't give up on this one. Before I have to wager on my offer, she immediately chimed in, "Yeah, I think that's exactly what we need."

Dear Reader, Thank you for reading Jasper and Evie's fun story. This is where the story originally ended. When I gave the book a new cover, I wanted to catch up with them to see how they are doing, so I added an extended bonus scene. If you want to see how they are doing after marriage, keep reading.

# Nineteen

## Evie

## A year after marriage

I'm not used to the way my silk pajama pants swish when I walk, but I still tiptoe barefoot over the castle marble floor on a quest for coffee. Not the gold-plated teacup version the staff insists on serving with dainty little biscuits. I crave the slosh-it-into-a-mug kind I used to sip in my trailer between takes.

Halfway to the kitchen, a butler intercepts me with a bow so deep it makes my stomach clench. "Your Highness." His eyes flick down to my bare feet, and he scowls as if I've strolled through the castle naked. "Breakfast is served in the dining hall. Her Majesty has requested your presence."

*I know!*

I know, because it's how we do it *every* Saturday, and I'm honestly tired of it.

I want to drink my coffee in the peace of my bedroom and not have to go through the dining room and be under a microscope to make sure I'm using the correct spoon, and my pinky finger has the correct angle as I tip my cup up. And don't get me started on the portions. I will never feel satiated by those tiny presentation-style portions. So what if I want cold cereal and a whole box of it?

I'm a whole grown adult!

I want to scream. Instead, I smile a brittle yet practiced smile. "Thank you." Pausing as I wait for the butler to turn, he stares at me, as if he's been assigned the task of not only informing me about breakfast but also ushering me back to the dining room.

When he doesn't budge, I resist a sigh and pivot a hard left into the Queen's flawless room.

She's already sitting there with her perfectly curled hair to support her perfect crown. She clears her throat as soon as I walk in. I curtsey and take my seat at the other end of the table. It's funny how my taste buds numb as soon as I'm in her company.

I no longer desire coffee, or anything...

Well, maybe Jasper would be great. He's in meetings this morning with official palace business, leaving me to dine with his mom alone, which wouldn't be so bad except even after a year of living here, I still feel like I hardly know her. To be fair, there's nothing wrong with her, and she's welcomed us into her home with open arms, but she's a hard person to bond with, as she's always surrounded by guards and servants. Not to mention, I'm terrified of saying something wrong.

The Queen looks at me over her teacup. "Did you happen to see the article about the palace on *The Morning Sprinkle*?" she asks, voice cutting. "They were speculating over some of your outfit selections and wondering if maybe you were concealing an heir."

The fork freezes in my hand. She says it casually, like she's commenting on the weather. To me, it's like a command I can't run away from. One that constantly beats in my brain like a drum: *Produce. Produce. Produce.*

"I'm still adjusting," I say softly, as if that can deflect the storm that's been gathering around me for months.

She hums a regal, knowing sound. "Of course. Our people look up to you to continue traditions. You understand that, right?"

*Do I?*

Because right now, I understand nothing. I don't understand why my life suddenly feels like it belongs to everyone but me. Why I'm supposed to sit here like porcelain, when all I want is to crawl back under the covers, drink coffee from a to-go cup, and breathe without the world watching.

I plaster on my rehearsed smile. "Of course."

Inside, my heart tightens like the door has been slammed on a cage and the lock keeps clicking tighter and tighter.

# Twenty

## JASPER

The silence of judgment is the loudest of all the silences.

Gritting my teeth, I try not to laugh, as I thought I was judged before when I was living in my gondola and stealing stale bagels to live. That was nothing compared to the stares of the parliament men in their haughty velvet coats, and the women in their chunky pearl necklaces.

Except now, I'm no longer the orphan people have pity on. I'm the prince, and next in line to be their future king. Which apparently means I'm supposed to sit here and nod while they dissect my life's choices.

"...an heir would stabilize the monarchy," the lanky robe-wearing man at the end of the table says. His voice is smooth as oil, but it still grates. "The people need assurance that the line is secure."

I keep my face still, trying to avoid letting them see that inside, I want to scream. Who even is this guy and why does he think he can make my personal life the topic of a very public meeting?

Because here's what they don't get:

I've spent my whole life without a family. No mother, no father, no name.

Just bouncing from one set of hands to another, learning quickly and young that you can't depend on anyone but yourself.

Sure, I got lucky with the find of life when I figured out who I really was, and I was also insanely blessed to convince Evie—the love of my life—to marry me.

So, I have family now.

Yes...I want kids, but it's not like I can order them with my Amazon Prime.

Some things take time.

I'm not even afraid of the diapers, the spit up, or then endless sleepless nights. *I want it all*. I want sticky hands tugging my shirt, and baseballs breaking my windows. I want to be the father I never had.

But I don't want the robed men in my business, staring down their pointy noses at me.

"Your Highness?" one of the older men prompts, as if I've been caught daydreaming. "Do you understand your duty?"

My jaw aches from how hard I'm clenching it.

I give them the polite smile. "Of course," I say as that's all I can manage. I hate that I'm forced to play the game.

By the time the meeting adjourns, I'm boiling under my skin. I burst out the doors, and storm down the hall, taking the time to glare at every portrait of some ancestor that's hung along the way. As if they could somehow have prevented this interrogation. When I finally make it back to our rooms, I'm wound tight.

Evie is already there, and her gaze connects with mine as soon as I fling the door open. Her eyes are wide, and if I only had one other word to describe her expression, it would be weary.

She feels this pressure too.

Something in me stutters. I know this isn't just my cage. It's hers too.

And heaven help me, I don't know how much longer either of us can keep smiling for them.

# Twenty-One

## Evie

By the time dinner rolls around, my anxiety is in full throttle.

*I can't do this again. Not tonight. I seriously just want to eat some greasy pizza and not care if I smear it all over my hands.*

Before the staff reaches me, I dig in the back of my closet for the single pair of street clothes I still own. I only have them because I've managed to keep them hidden from the cleaning staff. I pull on a hoodie and jeans and slip into sneakers. My heart hammers as I duck down the servants' staircase, all the while I'm praying no one sees me. It's a good plan as the staff should all be in the dining hall getting ready for our meal and not back here. For a second, I feel like myself again. Not a princess, not a symbol. Just a woman in sneakers wearing walking shoes to go downtown.

Somehow, I make my break away out the back door. Adrenaline pumps through my veins, and I take off sprinting into the night air. I breathe it in like it's oxygen I've been starving for, and I keep jogging down the hill toward town.

I find a little pizza shop with a neon sign buzzing faintly in the window. Inside, the tables are scratched, the floor is sticky, but I love it because it's the furthest thing from royal I've seen in a year. I order a greasy slice and sink into a booth by the window, where I proceed to eat my floppy pizza slice with my hands, stuffing my mouth so full I can barely chew.

For a few blissful minutes, I'm me again.

There's a white burst through the glass. I freeze with a half-eaten slice in my hand. Then there's another flash. I turn, and three paparazzi [MOU1] press their cameras almost against the window, lenses glinting like predators' eyes.

"Princess!" one shouts through the glass. "Are you pregnant yet?"

My blood turns to ice.

Can't I even eat a piece of pizza in peace?

Tears flood the backs of my eyes as I pull my hoodie over my head, drop the slice back onto the plate, and bolt for the door.

It's too late.

They're already circling, cameras strobing, questions pelting me like hail. *Where's the Prince? Why are you out alone? Trouble in paradise? Are you having twins?*

I can't answer these questions! Panicking, I run again, but with nowhere to go, I find myself running back to my prison—the palace. By the time I make it back, shame is clinging to me like smoke.

The guards don't meet my eyes as they let me back in. I can't tell yet if they are my friends, but I don't doubt this will be reported to the Queen. My heart sinks to a new low as I trudge back up the stairs to my room. I should be grateful for all the blessings in my life, and for being able to live in this beautiful castle, but sometimes...a girl needs to be herself.

The hall is empty, but I never feel completely alone in the castle. It's like the walls have eyes, and I hold my breath until I'm in my room. After I shut the door, I press my back to it, my chest rising and falling too fast.

This isn't the life I wanted.

I hate to complain because I love Jasper, but I'm suffocating here.

[MOU1]Singular and also plural

# Twenty-Two

## JASPER

I hear about it before I even see her.

A stiff-backed guard steps in front of me, and he spouts off with clipped words, "Her Highness was spotted in town, and paparazzi caught it."

The way he says it makes my chest burn.

I storm down the corridor, as my knuckles curl so tightly into fists. What was she thinking? She knows how the press is and how a single misstep becomes a wildfire. And she went out there alone? When I throw open our bedroom door, she's standing by the window with a tattered hoodie on, and her face pale. Startling at the sound of the door, she seems to jump.

"I'm just going to ask the question, but I'm not mad at you." My voice comes out rough. "Is it true you snuck out of the castle without guards?"

Her arms cross tight over her chest. "I just needed air," she says. "I needed to feel normal for five whole minutes—" she cuts herself off as her chin trembles.

My pulse slams against my throat. I want to hold her, to tell her I understand, but the truth is I'm worried. "I know I don't have to tell you how risky that was…" I step forward, searching her face for whatever it is that's really bothering her.

Her expression stays stone. "I know, but I was desperate."

"Desperate?" I choke as that seems a little dramatic. "What were you desperate for?"

Her lips part and a loud exhale slips out. "I've been trying to stay quiet and be grateful. I know you enjoy being here, and this is the first time you have ever had a family. I want so much to love it, but I feel more trapped here than I ever did in Hollywood."

The words hang heavy in the air. I look at her—the woman I love so hard it aches—and all I see is exhaustion. Stepping forward, I don't stop until I'm right in front of her, gazing into her eyes. One of my hands slides onto her hip. As I study the deep worry lines on her brow, I can't help but think I missed something. I've been so focused on proving myself to the council, to my mother, to the whole kingdom, that I haven't seen her suffocating.

"You think I want you caged, sweetheart? You think I want you miserable in these marble halls?" I shake my head, and go on, "No. I can't have you running off like that. Besides the fact that it's risky, it means you aren't happy. How did it get to this point?"

Her arms drop to her sides, and we stand here, both breathing hard. For the first time since the crown landed on my head, I don't feel like a prince. I feel like a man scared to lose his wife. Courage I should have gathered a long time ago crawls up my throat, and I spit out, "Evie, if this life isn't what you want, just say so. We'll do something else. It's not just about me and my family. It's about you and our family."

"I want this life," she rushes back as tears of honesty well in her eyes. "It's just, sometimes, I want to be able to do something normal. I don't think it needs to be on the news that I ate pizza."

A chuckle slips from my lips. Now that she's said it out loud, it sounds absurd. I totally understand where she's coming from, and I agree with her. I've been so wrapped up in my meetings and royal training that I almost missed the most important thing right in front of me. "I'm sorry I didn't see you were suffocating," I say, my voice low, rough with regret.

Her eyes soften, and before I can second-guess it, I lean down and capture her mouth with mine. She melts into me, fingers curling at the back of my neck, and when we part, her forehead rests against mine like she needs that tether just as much as I do.

"Then let's promise each other something," she whispers. "At the end of every day—no matter what—just us. Even if it's only for ten minutes."

My chest tightens in the best way. "Done. Just us."

"And... maybe breakfasts too?" she asks, almost shy. "I don't mind the dinners with your mom, but I'm not a morning person. It's hard for me to do this royal thing before I have coffee. Can we try for a while, just us, with to-go coffees, croissants, whatever we can sneak upstairs?"

I grin, brushing a kiss across the tip of her nose. "I'd like that more than you know."

We kiss again, deeper this time. When she pulls back, her smile tilts a little crooked, like she's confessing something forbidden. "I love being a princess," she admits softly. "But I want to be normal with you at least one day a week."

I cradle her face, my thumb sweeping across her cheek. "Then one day a week, you're not a princess. You're just mine."

Her smile glows with something stronger than any crown could give.

# Acknowledgements

I have to thank my kid for this one and her overactive imaginations. If you read the story, then you know this isn't your normal boss romance. I wrote the first act of this story several years ago when I needed a 10k words story for a boxset. I always wanted to finish it, but it seemed so silly, and even more slapstick than my normal romcoms. What did I do? I enlisted the help of my daughter to help me plot out the ending. She's six, and she loves to tell a good story too. If this story feels vastly different than many of my others, that is why. It has a quirky characters and Disney vibe, and I made a lot of memories writing it.

Thank you to Brenda. She's one of my editors, who happened to have extensive boat knowledge.

Rebecca, my other editor who is amazing at giving me the tough love when my stories need a lot more work, which is most of the time.

As always, thank you to the readers, and the entire bookish community. You guys are the reason I do this writing thing.

# About J.P. Sterling

J.P. Sterling grew up watching old reruns of Lucille Ball and Mary Tyler Moore and fell in love with wholesome entertainment and slapstick comedy. She loves leaning into the over-the-top humor and full circle moments, especially if it means the underdog gets to shine.

Aside from writing, she's also a wife and homeschooling mom, a holistic dietitian, a former college professor and lover of all-things dark chocolate.

*No swears. Just kisses. No Blasphemies. *

# Also by J.P. Sterling

***Christmas Shenanigans (All Standalones)***

Mingle All the Way

Tis the Season to Get Married

Let's Not and Sleigh We Did

***The Coffee Loft Series (All Standalones)***

Pardon My French Press

No More Mr. Chia Guy

Truly, Madly, Steeply Brew

***Sweet Hockey RomCom (All Standalones)***

The Pucker-Up Pact

Shot Through the Heart

Come and Get Your Glove

***A Modern Fairy Tale Series (All Standalones)***

Royally Rugged

***Bosses and Billionaires Series (All Standalones)***

Maid for my Billionaire Boss

Upcycling My Rig-Pig Boss

Kissed by My Billionaire Boss

Marooned with My Celebrity Boss

***<u>A Heart that Dances Series</u>***

Dancing on Broken Ankles

The Stars We See

A Heart that Dances

A Heart that Loves

***<u>Water and Stone Duet</u>***

Ruby in the Water

Lily in the Stone